THE WILLOW TREE

THE WILLOW TREE

Indian arrowhead

SUMMER REDFERN

COPYRIGHT © 2008 BY SUMMER REDFERN.

LIBRARY OF CONGRESS CONTROL NUMBER: 2008909793
ISBN: HARDCOVER   978-1-4363-8223-6
                   SOFTCOVER   978-1-4363-8222-9

The Willow Tree is strictly a work of fiction and does not negatively reflect in any way upon the towns, companies, institutions, law enforcement agencies, the armed services mentioned, nor upon any of the Native American tribes nor any other race or creed.

The names of the Tehran hostage crisis victims do not include Kai Harjo as he was not one of them, but we included him to make a social statement.

None of the incidents mentioned actually happened as they are simply figments of my imagination. I have taken some license with Native American names, customs, and folklore that may or may not be true. The name *Kai* is not an Osage word. It may be Native American, probably Navaho, but it means "willow tree" in this story.

This book was printed in the United States of America.

To order additional copies of this book, contact:
Xlibris Corporation
1-888-795-4274
www.Xlibris.com
Orders@Xlibris.com
54061

CONTENTS

Dedicated to my grandmother, a gracious lady
who taught me proper manners by her dignified unerring example.

Also to loving grandmothers, everywhere, who pick up the reins
when their daughters fail to care for their children.
We salute you.

Acknowledgments

I wish to thank the editors Jeanne Villaganasan and Ari Ben-Benjamin O. Mabansag for their excellence and help in making this book possible.

Thank you to the Willow Tree Foundation for their description of a willow tree. Visit their website at http://www.thewillowtreefoundation.org.

To the Native American website: http://www.firstpeople.us for the Osage Legend in which the old willow tree is addressed as Grandfather.

Note from the Author

The Willow Tree, written in the first person, facilitates understanding by the reader of the emotional turmoil experienced by each major character. It requires the reader to transition from one frame of mind to another. This takes a little more concentration than books written in the third person.

The reader may relate to the character or dislike the character but should come away with an understanding of how that person perceives his world.

The Willow Tree encompasses the 1980s when computer technology was just coming of age, and when racial integration was still stagnating in some of the rural areas of the South. In this tale, the legendary Grandpa Willow Tree shadows all of the human failings, misunderstandings, betrayal, forgiveness, and human kindness exhibited by each character as he stands steadfast in his old wisdom, omniscient yet unrevealing.

The Willow Tree Foundation describes the willow tree as follows:

"The willow tree is a relatively small tree without much trunk. Its branches are long and bending and give the appearance of being weak and fragile. Yet, when the storm rages, it is the willow tree that stands strong. Under the earth, the roots of the willow tree run long and wide; these roots hold the willow tree in place during the attacks from the violent winds. The deceptive branches are also strength for the willow tree. Without a large trunk, the willow tree branches are long and pliable. During the raging storm, the branches move and stretch with the wind. Ever bending, never breaking."

The Willow Tree

Wisdom of ages caught up in the willow
your catkins hang down as soft as a pillow.
The length of your age shown in the rings
the finest of times and those harder things.

Your medicine bodes for the body and soul
to mend all my years that have taken their toll.
I live by your words as I sit below
blossoms that comfort me sway to and fro.

Now dream me a dream of small children my own
to teach of your wisdom in which I was sown.
My life is opened by words of this book
trials I've taken, the memories I took.

Your peace you have given, as I have grown old
with shelter for all that come in from the cold.
Your limbs are woven in baskets of time
now comfort me more in this simple rhyme.

Love, Willow

Prologue

The stillness of the forest is broken as an armadillo rustles through the underbrush. As it wends its way, a thrush is startled, flapping its wings skyward. Dusk is settling as shadows of the past seem to prance about. Ghosts of mounted horsemen appear in the gloom, skirting the edge of a meadow and disappearing into the ether almost as quickly as they appeared.

Echoes of a former civilization permeate the region. Arrowheads gleam in the moonlit stream as a fawn sips the cool water. His mother, ever watchful, takes her turn. Mother and child of the forest turn silently and slip into its shelter to bed down beneath the thick overhanging boughs of a willow tree in a nest of flattened grass.

A flock of birds returns to the bushes, making a whistling sound as they settle in among the green branches. An owl awakes, shakes his wings, and lets out a mournful hoot. The owl takes flight as it spots a mouse on the forest floor and swoops down to catch it for its evening meal. Night settles over the scene as a cloud slips over the moon, leaving a profound darkness in its wake. All is silent as the forest sleeps.

Kai awakes to the sound of a siren, wailing in the night in a city as noisy as the forest is silent. He longs for the serenity of his youth although he is unaware of just what that entails. It is a primeval urge that has no immediate, recognizable symptom. He just feels that something is missing in his daily life, unable to define just what is lacking. Unable to sleep, he rises, stretching his long graceful frame as he reaches for the towel hanging on the back of the door and wraps it around his naked body in one quick motion.

He switches on the radio to catch the weather report. The forecast is for drizzle for the morning, clearing up by noon. "Another wet day," Kai murmurs, shutting the radio announcer off in midsentence.

After tending to his immediate needs, he dresses in his sweats and size 16 running shoes ready to take on the early-morning routine he has set for himself.

Kai stretches his six-foot, seven-inch frame in a move he has repeated ever since his six-year stint in the Marine Corps. The exercise routine he has perfected has kept his rock-hard body at the peak of perfection.

His dusky skin and long jet-black hair, tied back at the forehead with a strand of leather, could belong to any number of races except for the high cheekbones of a Native American.

Although he is not aware of his animal magnetism, he moves like a black panther as he pulls himself to his full height then ducks his head to clear the doorframe for his 5:00 AM run through the deserted morning streets of Smyrna.

Streetlights glow on each street corner, becoming a blur as Kai lopes along, his long legs stretching into giant strides in ever-quickening pace. The dark shadows seem filled with eyes as his footsteps echo across the empty streets, splashing through the many puddles of water along the way.

Night-blooming jasmine perfumes the morning air mixed with the pungent odor of honeysuckle that drapes the fence that is dripping with moisture from the rain that fell during the night. A warm southern breeze belies the fact that March has just arrived.

Dogwoods bloom in endless rows, overhanging his path as Kai retraces his steps and sprints back from whence he came. His cadence ever quickening as his long legs stretch to match his stride.

Kai is unaware of the car that is turning into his drive until he turns the corner and heads back to his apartment. The black minivan's lights dim as a tall, obviously, female figure emerges from the shadows. Her dark skin blends with the gloom. Only the light from her cigarette gives away her location.

Kai, now in defensive mode, slows his steps, not recognizing his visitor, until she speaks in her low southern drawl. "Jerome wants y'all to come by when you are done here. He wants that roof finished today."

"I have some important unfinished business before I can start on the roof, Tenika," he admonishes his sister. "You know that I have to fill out those forms for that job before I can come by. I reckon I can be there before noon."

Kai gives his only sister a bear hug, crushing her slender form to his. *How I love her, she is my only living relative,* he acknowledges. "Come on in while I change."

"I can't stay," Tenika replies regretfully. She misses her brother now that he no longer lives with her. "Jerome is waiting for me, and I have to get to work. We will get together later. I understand you asked Elena to marry you."

"A lot of good that did! She refuses even to consider it, but I will keep trying."

"Keep trying, Kai, I'll holler at you after work."

Disheartened now, Kai watches as Tenika slides into her minivan, her tall slender body, so like his own, reminds him of his childhood worship of his big sister. Tenika was always the leader, daring him to compete with her.

Tenika, the smart one, knew the answer to every question he could ask. *If only I knew all the answers*, Kai laments. *Maybe I could get Elena to marry me.*

Chapter 1

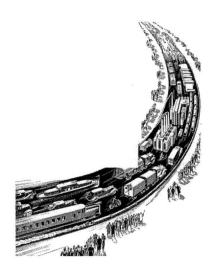

THE FAST LANE

Atlanta, Georgia
March 1984, Friday morning
Elena

"Um, what is that dreadful noise?" half-awake with my eyes closed, I grope on the bedside table until I find the alarm and smack my hand on the snooze button. "I just got to sleep." I open one eye to read the clock.

"I better get my sorry ass out of bed soon, that traffic will be bumper-to-bumper by six-fifteen."

A quick hot shower brings me somewhat to life. Taking the towel, I wipe off the foggy mirror and see the image of a young woman, with short red hair curling from the steam. A quick swish of mouthwash, I ignored my toothbrush, and promise a better job later. After a swipe of the comb through my tangles and a smudge of a bold apricot color on my lips, I find my clothes I had laid out from the night before on the chair. The navy blue uniform of the corporation: white lace on a high-necked blouse, navy skirt, and suit jacket, which I don with practiced efficiency, clip on the mandatory earrings, pull up my panty hose, and slide my feet into the closed-toed, high-heeled navy blue pumps.

"All for the sake of the corporate image," I murmur. "It's another day, just like all the other days and weeks of my well-ordered existence."

Expertly, I back my candy-apple red Volkswagen out of the driveway onto the roadway and head for the corner Dunkin' Donuts. I pick out an apple fritter and a steaming black coffee for the road and, just as quickly, slide back into the Volkswagen, and I am on my way.

A thick gray fog is hanging over Atlanta like a lover hugging the tall buildings. A fine mist is dripping moisture on my windshield. I flip on the wipers for a couple of noisy scrapes, decide I do not really need the irritation, switch them off again and tune my radio to the traffic report.

There is a wreck on I-75 that is blocking one lane. I-75 parking lot, as we commuters call it, delaying traffic almost to a standstill, reminding me of many similar drives into the city.

Construction of I-75 has been ongoing for some time, pulling the traffic into one or two lanes only. Progress has been slow, but worth it. Quoting from the *Atlanta Tribune*, "Soon there will be enough lanes for all the cars." Not, I think. There will just be more cars, and more traffic.

Atlanta and its suburbs are growing at an astounding rate. Urban sprawl is cutting down the trees and leveling the natural contour of the land. Hills become flat. Giant earthmovers are everywhere turning over the red southern soil. Neighborhoods seem to spring up overnight, bringing more cars and more congestion. Then even more roads will have to be built to accommodate all these new residents.

Cars jam the highway along with tractor-trailers moving like ants in a line. As the speed resumes, everyone starts to travel faster than conditions allow, skidding a little on the wet road. Too fast and they hydroplane into the next lane, injuring themselves and becoming one with the snarl. I watch as a yellow convertible slides sidewise and into the central median.

At least, it did not get in my way. Horns are bleating like so many sheep, and traffic slows, but just slightly. *Patience*, I think, *just be patient*. I am glad I'm not currently working all those short one-day temp jobs. Every day was a new adventure: finding the right office, finding a place to park, and going through all the aggravation of downtown one-way streets. I hope those one-day assignments are over for good.

Traffic is already starting to build as I turn onto I-285 for the forty-five-minute drive to Tucker. By making a deal with an oncoming pickup, I wave in appreciation and jerk ahead into the middle lane almost spilling my hot coffee. "Damn," I mutter but manage to take a bite of my fritter and a sip of coffee.

Somehow, the coffee begins its magic of calming my nerves as I shift into high and pull into the fast lane. The fast lane is where I belong. Here is safety from all those semis in the outside two lanes. *This is a lane I can really relate to: my lane, my city, my life.*

Mesmerized by the drive, my mind wanders to the offer (*plea* might be a better word) from my longtime boyfriend Kai who has just been hired by the State to work at the prison. I do not want to disappoint him, but how can I go live with him in that tiny, little one-stoplight town. "Well," he said with a grin, "Elena, we won't be living in town." (As if that were better!) "And, by the way, we gotta get married to live in state housing."

Just like that, he pops the question. No romance with that. None of this get-down-on-one-knee-will-you-marry-me. Nah, just gotta get married for the convenience of it no less. I am not certain I want to get married. Getting married for the convenience of it has never been on my agenda. The clock is not ticking yet. There will be plenty of time to get married. I have just begun my career. A baby would be sweet, but I am thinking later rather than sooner.

Of course, babies grow up and turn into ungrateful little monsters, or so one of my foster moms had scolded me when I was little. Maybe I was an ungrateful little monster! My babe would never be a monster, just a sweet little girl with curly red hair just like mine and a turned-up nose and a smile that would melt your heart.

As you have guessed by now, my name is Elena. I am twenty-four years old, single, a temporary word processor, all-around secretary, some time stenographer and girl Friday. I work for three temporary services. Summoned at the last moment, I fill in for an errant secretary that fails to show up for work, or I report for extra assignments. I am always on the run, sometimes for only half a day. One time for only three letters that needed typing. I got those done in fifteen minutes and then just sat there. "What else can I do for you?"

"That's all, you can go now if you like." The client had to pay for a half day anyway. It seemed like a waste of my time and their money.

My question is, How can there be so many Peachtree addresses in Atlanta all on a different Peachtree Road or Street, and where the heck am I supposed to park anyway? That information always seems to be lacking.

My next question is, Why do the companies that sell business machines always have typewriters that don't work? The last place I worked for was a typewriter company. My machine had a key that would stick and a platen that would jump off at the end of the row. I complained to the regular company typists, and they replied, "Oh, but you have the good one, you ought to try ours."

It seems like a manufacturer of typewriters would have the latest model for their secretaries to use.

I take on anything! I have no knowledge of shorthand, but I can remember at least two assignments where I just faked it. Taking notes, I used my photographic memory to make up for my lack of knowledge. One job lasted three days. Because the company did not want to use a recorder, I just took notes and typed them at home each evening. I cannot divulge their secret meeting, but the ramifications are scary. If you have a phone line, an outsider can snoop in your home without your knowing. Big Brother is watching, or at least listening.

Memory typewriters have been commonplace lately, and I have used them on many assignments. The advent of the computer has opened up a completely new technology for companies. At one of my long-term assignments, I used a Xerox computer that was a monster in size, but only displayed one line at a time. First, I used a boot floppy to start the computer and another floppy for the data. I transcribed an entire book for my boss using this dinosaur, which was difficult to edit. When I left, I had to come back because nobody knew how to edit the floppies.

My latest temporary but long-term assignment is in Tucker, which I simply adore. At least there is adequate parking, my supervisors ignore me, and I have an office all to myself where I can work without interruption. It would be lonely in there except for the fast pace. I process data and produce pages of statistics for the company as well as letters for various major bigwigs in Atlanta. My main obstacle is knowledge of how to address them all by the appropriate title as honorable this and honorable that.

I have had to become familiar with what paper everyone uses and what syntax they each have in mind, retype their edited material, and get it back to them on time.

Everyone on the entire floor uses my expertise, which makes me feel important to the welfare of this company. Pride is probably unwarranted because if I were not here, someone else would be. That is the nature of this business. As companies train more word processors, my value decreases.

I have no more time to consider this as my off-ramp approaches, and without a second thought, I start to cut across lanes of the fast-moving traffic that by now has become a solid mass. A horn behind me blares as I cut in front of a grassy-green minivan whose mousy-haired driver gives me the finger. "Same to you, sweetie," I mouth as I weave across the far lane and make the turn up the ramp onto North Lake Drive.

A sigh escapes my lips as I wait for the light to change. The car in front does not seem to notice the green light, so I beep my horn, and we start to move again. One more block and I turn my car into the parking lot.

Glancing in the mirror, I run my fingers through my hair, apply more lipstick, which has worn off from the coffee, lock the Volkswagen and slide out. "The drive was not so bad today," I say to no one in particular, "but this afternoon is going to be a hot one."

The car will be a furnace by the time I make the return home. The lack of air-conditioning will make for a hot ride. At least it's Friday, which is good because there is no work tomorrow, but bad because traffic will be jammed. It is worse on Friday than any other day of the week, and rush hour starts earlier.

I am slowing down a bit as I emerge from the little red bug, lock my door, and head for the spacious, cool headquarters of this regional office. It is an imposing building, not tall, just eight stories of local-quarried granite tucked into the hillside of North Lake as though the granite were part of the surrounding rock.

Spring this year seems more like summer. The flowering pear trees have finished blooming, and the wind is trailing the white petals as snow across the parking lot that is relatively empty as I walk toward the entrance. My early arrival is deliberate, as it is the only way to survive the traffic that builds on the highways after 7:00 AM. It is convenient to have a parking lot this close to a building for a change.

"Hi, Elena," a cheery voice behind me calls, which I recognize as Jillian's. She is dressed in a similar navy blue suit. Jillian is a beautiful black girl who works on the fifth floor as a receptionist. I invite her to have coffee with me in the first-floor lunchroom.

"No, ma'am, not today, there is an early meeting on fifth." Jillian breezes off without another word. *Hmm, I wonder why I did not hear about it!* Of course, I am left out the loop a lot in the cave I work in. I am distracted for a moment, but think, *Oh, well, if they wanted me there, I would have received a memo.*

Pouring a cup of the black inky-looking stuff that passes for coffee in the makeshift lunchroom, I head to the elevator for fifth floor. Other early arrivers share the tiny space. Some nod, and others look straight ahead, ignoring my presence. All are dressed in similar attire: suits, ties, briefcases for the men, who have a newspaper tucked under their arms, and navy blue or silver suit jackets and skirts for the women all with the mandatory earrings and closed-toed, high-heeled pumps. We could all be store manikins, I think, for business fashion departments. As I reach fifth floor, most of the manikins have departed to various areas. I quickly unlock my office, put away my personal belongings, and sit on my designated chair in front of the large computer ready to boot it up. Another busy day is about to begin, and I want to get heads-up on it.

This has been the best job I have found. I do not have to carry on unnecessary conversations all day. I get to work on a high-tech computer, an automated Dictaphone that activates by a call-in from the telephone system and a new invention called a fax machine. This allows me to send written material to another fax machine in another office anywhere in the United States. Someday, the paper from the fax and the copier need to use regular paper, if possible, rather than burning it into the sheets of semitransparent copies that our machines currently produce.

I have an office all to myself, not like some of the other jobs I have had where the desks are close together, and the office buzzes with conversation and machine noise. It is completely private. No one else enters this domain except me. The various secretaries pick up corrected copies that I leave in a file attached to my door. I think I could work here forever.

Chapter 2

GRANDPA WILLOW TREE

Marietta, Georgia
April 1984, Friday morning
Kai

    This housing form for the State I am filling out asks for race. Who am I? *Estelusti* is the name Granny gave as our race: Black Native American. I guess I will put Native American. That is how I filled out my form for the Marine Corps. I really do not want to put Black because I intend to be married to a white girl, and in some areas of the South, that may cause controversy. My pa was black; Granny was Osage, Native American. She was my mama's mother.

Granny, as was proper for an Earth Clan woman, was married first to a member of the Sky Clan and, after the proper mourning of her husband's death, to a Black Creek Muskeg.

I favor my granny: lighter skin more beige than black. My hair is straight and long but not as long as when I was a child. Granny used to plait it for me into two braids.

Granny told me that she sat under a willow tree praying, "Grandpa Willow Tree, send me a daughter that I might have someone to help me in my old age."

Grandpa Willow Tree must have taken pity on this forty-eight-year-old woman, past her prime for bearing children, as she bore a child—a daughter she called Mina (Osage for "first daughter").

Her daughter was her pride. Tall and proud, too proud actually, who thought she knew more than her aging mother did. Mina ran off, and lived with my pa when she was only fifteen and got pregnant. Granny told her, "You laid your bed in that man's lodge, now sleep in it!"

Mina's firstborn was a daughter whom Pa named Tanika. "Funny name for a girl," Granny said because Pa had named her. Granny always yearned for a son, so she sat again under her Willow Tree and pleaded, "Oh, Grandpa Willow Tree, I never had a son to carry our name. Please send down a son for my daughter, Mina, that I may at least have a grandson."

Mina got pregnant again, and Grandpa Willow Tree sent her a baby boy that Granny named Kai, to honor the Willow Tree. Pa was furious that they named me Kai without consulting him, and he beat Mina. Pa had no qualms about hitting a woman, and he hit Mina regularly when he was displeased. Mina got tired of his abuse and ran away. She left Tanika and me with Granny.

Granny raised us when Mama ran off. She would tell us how beautiful our mother was, tall and strong, and that Mina loved us very much. Mina, she said, was watching over us from afar. "She can't come back now because of your Pa," Granny explained. "I will ask Grandpa Willow Tree to send her back to you when it is safe."

Pa never paid much attention to Tanika or me. We hated him from driving our mother away. Pa sneered, "Ain't that somethin'! That baby mama don' want her chile." He never knew how much that hurt. Rejection and shame followed that remark, which he made loudly and more than once. "Pay him no mind," Granny always said. "We are a proud people, so hold your head up high. He never treated your mama right. Kai, you are my chile, and Tanika is my chile until Mina returns."

Tanika still remembers Mina, or thinks she does, but I was just a babe. Pa was black and only lived long enough to make our lives miserable. Pa died the year I turned eleven in a drug deal that went bad. Life was much better without him.

I never knew my grandfather Flight Harjo, Granny's Black Creek husband. He had already passed away before I was born. I had little male influence in my life while growing up unless you can count Grandpa Willow Tree. Sitting under that tree, I was content. It was my shelter from the rain. He comforted me when I was sad. Grandpa Willow Tree listened to all my childhood woes without so much as a reprimand for my foolishness. He sang to me when the wind blew. *I loved that old tree.*

Granny was strict, and Grandpa Willow Tree gave up several of his limbs as switches to use when I did not obey her. Granny never used a switch on Tanika.

When we were sick, Granny used willow tea to ease our fever, and chew sticks made of willow to clean our teeth.

Whatever Granny planted grew. She would talk to the plants as they were growing. She knew the native folklore and brewed her own medicines. Tanika and I never had a doctor visit. Granny did not find a need for modern medicine.

We never had much or expected much in those hills of North Carolina. We were satisfied with what we had. Deer and other forest creatures would come into the yard. Occasionally, a brown bear visited us. Although we seldom saw him, we knew he was there. He rummaged through our garbage, scattering it around. Granny would fuss and pick it up again. She never complained about any creature.

We did not have electricity or running water. An outhouse was out back for our needs. A lantern lighted our cabin. A woodstove in the kitchen was all Granny needed to heat the water from the well for our bath and to cook up the vegetables she grew. We fished in the stream for trout.

Granny ground acorns and made acorn cakes. She picked wild mushrooms in the forest and dug roots to add to her stew. She bought flour from town and made sourdough bread from a recipe that her mother had given her. Tanika and I ate everything she cooked. We were not allowed to complain no matter how meager the meal.

Granny was full of love and life, and we loved her as our mother. I never saw Granny unhappy. She accepted the world as she found it. If she had a problem, she dealt with it.

We learned many fables about the Willow Tree as we lived in its shadow. My memory is not exact, but one of my favorites went something like this:

Little One wanted to know the meaning of life. While on his quest, he stumbled and fell into a pool of water and saved himself by clinging to the roots of a willow tree.

32

The willow tree was old, and Little One called out, "Grandpa Willow Tree, how should I live to become as old as you?" Grandpa Willow Tree answered, "You must be like the willow: bending in the wind, keeping your roots centered in Mother Earth, and keeping your eyes focused on Father Sky. You must shelter the animals and weep for the unfortunate. You must cling to life until the end and be in perfect harmony with Mother Earth and Father Sky.

(Osage Legend)

When Pa died, I really expected to have Mina come back to us, but Grandpa Willow Tree must not have answered Granny's request, or maybe he said, "Not yet, wait until the time is right."

After Pa died, Granny had no more reason to stay in North Carolina, so she took Tanika and me back to her home in Missouri to be with her older sister. We took cuttings from Grandpa Willow Tree with us to Missouri, which we planted there. Three willow trees sprang up from those cuttings. Willows grow quickly, and soon Granny had three tall trees, one for herself, one for Tanika, and one for me.

Although the branches were from Grandpa Willow, my tree was a poor substitute for him maybe because it was so young.

After studying in class about the Trail of Tears, I asked Granny why her family never had to move to the Oklahoma territory. She told me the story about how her grandfather and grandmother, toting a child on her back, rode ponies from Missouri to North Carolina, a very long trip on horseback. Most of the clans and many of her relatives remained in Missouri. Granny told me it was very unusual for an Osage to be in North Carolina. Most Native Americans from this area are Cherokee or Creek.

Several families from both the Earth Clan and Sky Clan accompanied my great-great-grandparents, and the little group hid in the hills. Granny was the youngest of four children, three girls and a boy. The boy and one of the girls died in a fire that consumed their cabin. Granny and one sister escaped. Granny's only surviving older sister married a man who returned to Missouri.

When Granny was fourteen, she was married to a much older man that her mother chose for her from the Sky Clan. Clan membership regulated marriage. Osage Earth Clan members always married Sky Clan members, so every Osage child was the product of a union of Sky (Father) and Earth (Mother).

This union only lasted ten years and produced no children. When Granny's Sky Clan husband died, she went into mourning for many moons.

Her second husband, my grandfather, was Flight Harjo. Granny was proud that she had chosen him herself. My paternal great-grandfather was the son of a freed slave who took a Creek widow for his wife. He took the Creek name of Harjo. As Pa never married Mina, our mother, Tanika and I used the last name Harjo.

Both Tanika and I finished high school. Tanika was the smart one and went on to college with a scholarship. I was the slow one, but I made my way to a Marine Corps recruiter who talked me into signing up for six years.

The corps made me into a man. During my tour of duty, I served in Tehran at the U.S. Embassy. Not being able to fire our guns, terrorists kidnapped us and held us hostage for 444 days. After our ordeal with the devil, I was shipped State side, but I will never forget those days of terror.

I feel, until this day, that we should have fired our weapons. We would have all been dead, but it would have proved that the USA does not surrender to terrorists! If I had not had that dreadful experience, I might have re-upped. Although the Carter administration attempted to rescue us, I felt that the corps had let us down. Maybe I should have re-upped. I would not be in a bind now for a job.

After Tanika finished college, she married Jerome a black student she met in her class and moved to Atlanta. Both Jerome and Tanika got jobs with the State. Jerome is a probation officer, and Tanika works as a counselor for Defax.

Granny died while I was in the marines, so I moved to Atlanta to be near Tanika. I wish I had been home for Granny's funeral. Tanika had Granny's body shipped back to North Carolina where they buried her beneath Grandpa Willow Tree. Later, Tanika paid to have a stone placed on the grave. Someday, I want to return to visit Grandpa Willow Tree and Granny's resting place.

I met Elena six months ago while on a job as a security officer. She was working in a bank on what she called a temporary assignment. Stunned by her beauty and flaming red hair, it took me, a hardened marine, several days before I had enough courage to ask her out. Since then, we have dated regularly. Elena is more intelligent than I am. I wish I had her fantastic memory.

Elena's skin is soft and white, with freckles across a turned-up nose, and eyes the color of emeralds—a real Irish beauty. Tall for a woman, she is six feet in heels. I still have her beat by almost seven inches. Her legs are long, slender, and gorgeous. When she smiles, I feel like the sun is shining. She is my ideal woman. I would like to be with her always.

I will never treat my woman as Pa treated Mina. Pa was mean as a bear. I feel that I have insulted the bear with that comparison. He just used Mina. He never intended to marry her. She was just his baby mama. No wonder she ran off. That is not how I will treat Elena. I will follow Granny's example. She taught us respect for marriage and commitment. No baby mamas for me, Elena deserves the best.

Security is my first job after the marines. I have worked for banks, hotels and the Greyhound Depot, which was not too bad until the drivers went on strike. Some of the hotel jobs, especially on Lucky Street, were the pits. Why anyone would name it Lucky, I do not know. Lucky Street is one of the worst neighborhoods in downtown Atlanta.

The security firm gave me a position as sergeant. The pay is a little better than that for a regular security officer. Sometimes I have to supervise other officers, but most of the time sergeant is just an honorary position because I was a marine.

My lack of college education has prevented me from getting any higher-paying jobs. I have been doing odd jobs recently to make ends meet and to save a little for when I get married.

As Tanika and Jerome work for the State, they suggested I get a State job, which has benefits, benefits that I will need to raise a family. I put in for highway patrol, but there was no opening. The highway patrol took my application and my test score and encouraged me, saying my Marine Corps training would put me at the top of the list. In the meantime, I have applied and been accepted as a correctional officer. I feel qualified for either job.

While I am waiting for the State, I have been building a garage for Tanika and her husband Jerome. The job is just about finished except for the roof. Roofing is hot work in this Atlanta sun. Starting early in the morning before the main heat of the day, I work for a few hours. Then I have to wait until it cools in the evening to finish.

It is going to be hot today, not like that cold reception I got from Elena last night when I asked her to marry me. *What is up with her anyway?* She sure as hell was hot enough in bed. Maybe she thinks I am not good enough or smart enough to make a good husband.

I may not be as intelligent as she is, but I am strong and I work hard. I cannot imagine my life without her in it. Since I have met her, I have tried in every way possible to live up to her expectations. I do not know what else she wants from me. It is time for us to get married. Man, I am ready to settle down and raise some young'ns.

All my life, the only thing I have wanted is to have a family. Much of my insecurity stems from Mama abandoning us. I need someone who cares for me, who will stay with me and will care for my children. Elena, as caring as she is, will be the ideal wife and mother. I love her, and I think she loves me. Wanting to stay in Atlanta is just a childish dream. She could live anywhere and be happy if she puts her mind to it.

Well, I have to stop thinking and get this job finished. My sister is going to yell her head off if this roof is not finished by tomorrow night. I'm a-fixin' to call Elena tonight and see if I cannot convince her to marry me. Maybe if I am persistent enough, she will give in.

Chapter 3

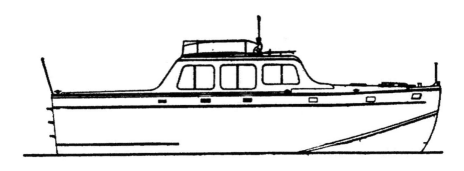

LITTLE RICHARD

Tucker, Georgia
Friday morning
Elena

    Friday's schedule begins with a rush. There are papers outside my door that have been proofed and ready for me to edit. Picking up the stack of papers, I barely reach my desk when the Dictaphone beeps, a tape comes across from the machine, and I begin my day dressed to the nines although no one can see me in my hideaway cave except for this monstrous computer that hums and shakes and has a mind of its own. I've named it Cyclops. Cyclops does what I tell it to most of the time. He or it is not all that bad, and he keeps me company as I type away, oblivious to the outside world. There is no window in this cave, just Cyclops and me.

There is no time for daydreaming today. It's Friday, the end of the week, and there is more work than I can finish. I am no slouch. Cyclops and I can put in 110 keystrokes per minute without breaking a sweat. The Dictaphone keeps beeping as Cyclops and I finish a ninety-nine page article about computer systems. All those figures and stats are making my head swim. I hit Ctrl P and send everything to the printer while I retrieve that tape from the insistent Dictaphone. The phone rings just as I grab the tape and shove it into the player. Cyclops keeps sending data to the printer as I pick up the phone. "Way to go, Cyclops!"

"Corporate Headquarters," I trill, "Elena speaking."

The gruff voice at the other end is scolding, "Where is my report?"

"I heard your secretary pick it up about fifteen minutes ago. Maybe she took her break first."

"Humph, OK!"

It is time for a short break while Cyclops finishes. My mind wanders back to the problem at hand. So why, after dating this guy for six months, does he want to marry me and take me away from Atlanta? I am perfectly happy here in the fast lane. When he first said he was going to work for the State, I was thinking highway patrol, which I considered a glamorous job. Working as a correctional officer was never on the agenda until now. There must be a prison here in Atlanta where he could work.

Well, back to Cyclops, he is ready for more, the Dictaphone is beeping again, the phone is ringing, and I have a ton of work to finish. With the typing, correcting, printing and ringing, there is no time to get lonely. Cyclops is humming away as though he just cannot wait to print again. I load in envelopes and push Ctrl P, and start printing all those important names for the mayor and all those officials. There will be hell to pay if I did them wrong.

By 4:00 PM, I have my work completed and the desk cleared. I now have a few moments to myself. "Cyclops, old boy," I ask my companion, "How can I consider that marriage proposal? I would have to give up this job and give up the perfect house I managed to find. I really love him, Cyclops. Do I really want to stay single forever, and what about children? I would like a couple, but why do I have to choose? Maybe what I need is a normal relationship with one of those computer nerds down the hall, but they all seem so full of themselves. Maybe I could ask one out for coffee. One of them is good-looking in a nerdy sort of way. If he would lose those horn-rim glasses, he'd look even better."

Cyclops just sits and hums as if he knows what I am talking about.

It is 4:15 PM, and I get a knock on the door. Jillian, looking a little tired, looks around and asks, "Who were you talking to?"

"Cyclops," I answered inanely.

"You're a strange one. What could you possibly have to say to that darned old computer? I just stopped by to tell you about the meeting we had this morning" she whines. "We are all going to be laid off at the end of the month!"

"What do you mean by all?"

"Well, the temps on third and fifth. It seems they are cutting back in Denver, and a bunch of permanent employees wants to transfer to Atlanta. We will all be out in the cold."

"Don't worry, it doesn't get that cold in Atlanta," I console with a confidence I do not feel. "I know they are hiring at Coca-Cola. They have some neat computer jobs. Irv will find us something there." (Irv is the supervisor at one of the temporary services who has sent me out on some good assignments.)

Mentally, I groan because I have to change jobs again, drive downtown, or take some of those short-term assignments that I really hate. And what about Cyclops? I will really miss him. Oh well, water off a duck's back, we will survive.

Lost in thought, I find my car and I was right—the steering wheel is too hot to touch. The little Volkswagen has no air-conditioning, and the ride home will be brutal. Back on I-285, the traffic is at a standstill. What took me forty-five minutes this morning will take at least two hours at this rate to drive back to North Cobb.

A girl in the car ahead of me has a book out that she is gazing at while nibbling an apple. I decide to get out my lipstick and reapply it. The face in the mirror looks older somehow. Where did those little wrinkles around my mouth come from? Same curly hair, too bad it is soaking wet from the heat.

I am glad I do not wear makeup—it would be running down my chin by now. The shower is going to be a real necessity when I get home. I retrieve my toothbrush from the visor where I keep it handy for just such occasions and absentmindedly start chewing on it.

Heat builds up in the car as in a sauna at this slow pace. The sun is brutally beating down on the roof, and I am burning the arm I have perched on the open window ledge. It is nice to have a suntan but not just on my left arm. I never could see lying in those tanning beds deliberately burning my skin. As redheaded as I am, burning is the only word for it. Other people tan. I just turn red, burn, or freckle.

Impotently, the snarl of cars, semis and frustrated drivers barely creeps along for the first hour. I look up and find a big boat in front of me. "Little Richard" it says on the back. "Well, *Little Richard*, you are blocking my view." Who the heck would be hauling a boat this size in rush hour? There is no chance of getting out from behind *Little Richard* during the next hour either. All lanes are blocked, no getting into the fast lane if it could be called that today. *Little Richard* is all I can see anyway.

I am beginning to hate anything called Richard, especially an oversized craft that I recognize as anything but little. Finally, the ramp to I-75 north appears, and sure enough, *Little Richard* is still ahead of me, hauling his fat ass up the ramp.

I-75 parking lot is really one today. Stop, start, stop, start, no wonder I have had to have the clutch replaced twice. I guess I should get a car with an automatic shift, but I really love this little red bug. It is so easy to maneuver.

Wow! *Little Richard* just turned off on Windy Hill, and the road is again visible. Traffic is not much better, but at least now, I can see all that merging cars and trucks ahead.

My hands have finally cooled off, the steering wheel is at least touchable, and the traffic smell has gotten better. I am changing into my almost-home mode, which is like an autopilot. Home is just a few minutes away.

My mind wanders again to Kai. Will he call tonight? What will be my answer? Jeez, I do not want to leave my new home behind, but I guess this would be the perfect time to leave if my job is ending. And I really do love him. Oh, why can't life be simple? I guess I fear the unknown. Life has been such a pattern these last three years, same routine, a no-brainer. Are there any jobs for me there? I sure as hell cannot just sit home and keep house. *A correctional officer cannot make that much.* How will he support me?

I guess I could get rid of this jacket in this heat. At least in the country, I could get by with jeans and a T-shirt. The thought lingers, but I'm not certain I am ready for the rural life. I got enough of that as a kid in all those they-could-care-less foster homes.

The last one I ran away from did not even bother to look for me. I was almost eighteen anyway. Jobs were not that plentiful for a seventeen-year-old. I worked all the fast-food places I could find in Wyoming and then hitchhiked with a trucker headed for Atlanta. I fell in love with this city on first sight. Although I was a scared kid at the time, now that I have come this far, I never want to leave.

A cooling breeze tries to dry me off as I step out of my car. Home at last, I look at my house. *Is it that fantastic here? Yeah, it is!* This modern split-level in a quiet neighborhood with minimal yard does not require much upkeep. The flowering pear trees that surround the yard have finished blooming, but the roses I planted last spring are now opening their petals, nodding their heads as if to say, "Cheer up, this is your home. Stay here."

I answer in a grateful tone, "You can bet on it! I can't leave all this behind." I unlock the door, kick off my shoes, and head for the shower.

Chapter 4

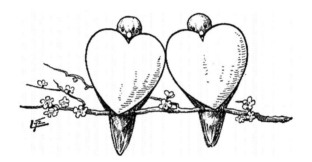

THE PROPOSAL

Marietta
Friday afternoon
Kai

All I can think about today is Elena. This roof is still not finished, but I promise myself I will have it done tomorrow. This old towel comes in handy to wipe the dirt and sweat from my face. I am going to have to get this long hair cut by the time I take that State job. There is plenty of time after I get the roof finished. It will not be as short as that first cut in the marines. Man, they shaved me bald. For a young longhaired punk as I was, that cut was really a shock. I thought I'd been scalped. It taught me a valuable lesson—hair is not *anything*. Hair does not make the man. If they want me bald, I can be bald, no sweat.

Granny used to tell me that the men in her Osage Clan used to shave their heads, all except a small patch that they wore long. They were tall fierce warriors that struck fear in the hearts of many other tribes. Many of her clan, she said, were over six feet tall, some even as tall as seven feet. Granny herself was tall for a woman, and I am six feet seven. Being this tall has been an advantage in many ways. I do not know if I strike fear in the hearts of others as Granny told it, but my height and muscle have kept many men from picking a fight with me. Even when I was a kid, most of the bullies in school left me alone. I am more of a lover than a fighter anyway. That's what I tell Elena.

Calling it quits for today, I drive to my apartment in Smyrna. The traffic is bumper-to-bumper as rush hour is still on for I-75. The drive back to North Cobb later should be better. At least I should be at my apartment in time to catch Elena home. Just as soon as I clean up, I'll call her. That way, she won't be waiting for me so long. She always has a bird if I am not there on time.

My apartment is hot and filled with dirty clothes. I have not taken the time to wash them. Dishes from the last meal are still in the sink. If I am to get Elena to come here with me tonight, I have to put these dishes in the dishwasher and at least hide my clothesbasket.

I turn on the air-conditioning, rinse the dishes, and put them in the dishwasher. I need the water for my shower, so the dishes will just have to hide there until I get more time. *A wife would be nice.* She could do this for me.

Something Tanika said today made me think of Mina. That old song and dance about Mina finding us must be a crock. I would not have the first idea of where to look for her, but something in me feels missing. It is hard to explain. Even though Granny loved us, I have always had a niggling doubt. Why would a mother not want her child? She could have run away and taken us with her.

"Oh, Elena, please marry me and give me a child. I would never run away from a child of mine. We will stay together, no matter what. If you will be here for me, I will always be here for you, I promise!

"I know we have different backgrounds. You like the city, and I prefer the country life. You are not a southern belle, and I am not the typical white southern gentleman, but if we have each other, that is all we will need."

Chapter 5

Mina's Journey

Ellsworth Air Force Base, South Dakota
1983
Mina

Sometimes I feel as though my children are crying for me. I hear their voices calling, "Mama." They must be all grown up by now. Maybe they even have their own families.

Finding my daughter, Tanika, and my son, Kai, has become an urgent quest. Mama had me leave because she could not stand the beatings I was getting from that brute. There was no safety for me as long as he was alive.

I knew where my children were when Mama had them. I came and watched them from a distance when they were little. They seemed so happy with Mama that I did not want to interfere because I knew she wanted them as much as I did. They loved Mama as I did, but I was just too young and too foolish to help. I wish I had taken my children with me. Now I have lost them.

I was never the daughter Mama wanted me to be, just willful and stubborn, and see where it got me. I was just a baby too at the time, although I did not realize it. Babies should not be making babies. That is why Grandpa Willow did not listen when I asked him where my babies were. When I went back, Mama had moved, and I lost track of everyone.

By that time, I had my new life in the air force. Grand Forks, North Dakota, was my first base after boot camp. There was a missile wing, a bomber wing, and a tanker wing there. The missiles have long-range nuclear capabilities. I have not had any experience with the missile silos although some of my friends have. They stay out in the silo for several days and nights and then have time off.

Who would have imagined me, a southern girl, in that cold place? Snow and ice that first year were so much different from what I had experienced.

My job as a jet engine mechanic was amenable even if the climate was not. I was shocked when they decided to train me to fix these big jets. Basic training was hard. At least it conditioned me, as I was soft and out of shape. I was older than most of the young women in basic, and they showed me up more than once.

When I enlisted for six years, I got a couple stripes. I outrank some of the men, which gave me a little advantage. Some of them had to take orders from me, so I got out of some of the dirty jobs.

I miss my children, but it helps to keep busy. Mother took the best care she could of them. I hope they listened to her better than I did. The foolishness of my teenage years has brought me so much sorrow. Older now and wiser, I will not let my emotions ruin my life. This life has been so different from anything I have ever done. I like the structure and the order of it. Most things go according to plan. My life has had no structure or purpose until now.

Love came knocking the second year in Grand Forks. Working in the parts department, I met Mark, a crew chief, who just happened to come in for a part himself. He usually just sent one of his crew for the parts, but he was in a hurry that day. We did not have much time to become acquainted. We met again in the canteen and spent some time together. I was not looking for a boyfriend, but his smile and sense of humor won me over. We were just friends for a while until he got enough nerve to ask me for a date.

It was a New Year's Eve party. I will never forget that first date. When everyone was singing "Auld Lang Syne," I gave him a hug and wished him Happy New Year. He leaned down to kiss me, and the sparks flew. I kissed him back with so much enthusiasm that he almost fell over.

Mark and I were married after a rather long engagement of two years. I was reluctant to get married after that teenage nightmare, but Mark wanted a child and I gave in. Mark was amazed when I told him the story about Tanika and Kai. He is very much in favor of finding them, which makes me love him even more.

Kai, if I can find him, will be so surprised to have a new brother. I always think of Kai first because he was my baby when I left, and it broke my heart to leave him. Tanika was already two, and I miss her, but I miss Kai more.

I had almost three more years to go before my second tour of duty was up, and finally I became pregnant with Flight. We named him after my dad, Flight Harjo.

I got my GED before I enlisted, but I would have liked to go back to school. Mark preferred I be a stay-at-home mom, so that is what I did.

My new baby boy was two before that could happen, and the air force discharged me. Mark re-upped for his fourth tour of duty because he is a career man. Now that I have this child, I am glad I can be home with him. Being a mother can be a full time job.

We are here now at Ellsworth Air Base at Rapid City, South Dakota. It is not quite as cold here, and the scenery is outstanding. Rapid City has this rather strange climate. It can snow and be cold one day, but the next day, warm winds come up from the South, melt the snow and warm up the atmosphere, so it feels as spring. Rapid City is in the piedmont of the Black Hills Range of South Dakota. Although hills surround us, our elevation is rather flat. There is plenty of room here for an airbase.

Mark is still working as crew chief. The air force keeps upgrading his education. Ellsworth is the home of the B-52 bombers. There are rumors that soon a larger bomber will replace these, and the B-52s phased out. Mark says he is ready for that to happen.

Rattlesnake
(from 2 to 8 ft.
long, according
to the kind)

We are having trouble with rattlesnakes here at the base. It has been rainy, and the prairie rattlers and bull snakes have become a nuisance. Sometimes they get into the house. I was surprised one day to have one in my living room. Prairie rattlers are not that aggressive, but they will strike if provoked. Their bite is deadly. I have to be careful with my little boy. He cannot just go out to play. I have to be on guard for the snakes.

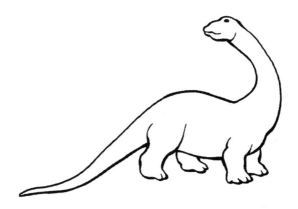

A statue of a large dinosaur stands on the hill overlooking the town of Rapid City. We visit it often as Flight likes to sit on it and pretend he is a cave man. Near Rapid City is the famous Mount Rushmore monument. It is amazing how they could carve this large outcropping of rock to make those huge faces. The road leading up to Mount Rushmore is nothing but hairpin curves, switchbacks and tunnels.

Near Mount Rushmore is a carving that depicts Chief Crazy Horse. This interests me because of my Native American heritage. It does not look like much yet, but the plans look interesting. The huge project will take years to complete.

In addition, northwest of Rapid City are the historic towns of Deadwood, with its Boot Hill and tales of Calamity Jane and Buffalo Bill Cody. Up the mountain two miles is the mile-high city of Lead, home of the Homestake Gold Mine. Tunnels extend deep into the earth to bring up the gold ore. I understand that on the average, it takes a ton of rock to recover four-tenths of an ounce of gold, which is about enough to cover the tip of your little finger.

The surrounding hills remind me of my home in North Carolina. The pine trees whisper to me just as they did as a child. Someday, I hope I can get back to that warm southern climate.

I often think about Grandpa Willow Tree, if he is still guarding that Bee Tree Creek up on the Cherokee Trail. The creek there is shallow but becomes faster whitewater as it continues on its route. That old tree clung to the bank of the creek, his roots firmly anchored in the red clay. He must be very old if he is alive at all. I will get back there someday if I can. I miss that old homeplace and that old tree.

Although I have attempted to get in touch with my family, I cannot find them. They were in North Carolina the last time I knew. Now that I have more free time, I think the time is right to continue my search. I do not see why it is going to be that difficult other than finding a place to start.

Mark and I are so glad we found each other. He is so good to me. Love is not just sexual attraction or looks as I thought it was as a foolish young girl. Mark is not a handsome man, but looks are not that important to me. It is what is in his heart that counts.

Chapter 6

THE PROMISE

North Cobb
Friday Afternoon
Elena

There is nothing like a shower to make up for a sweaty drive. Dripping wet, I step out and reach for a towel, and the phone rings. It usually rings when I am in the shower. It seems to know I cannot reach the darn thing. Its ring is insistent as I leave a puddle on the floor, still dripping wet and hurry to answer it. What is there about a phone that makes you answer it? I can never just let it ring.

"Kai, what's up—Oh!—you are on your way over—how long—well, maybe in twenty minutes. See you, bye." Looking again at that face in the mirror, like the wicked witch in Snow White, I am certainly not the fairest in the land, but I guess I will do.

I redo my lips, run a comb through my wet hair, pick out a little pink number from my closet, slip my bare feet into sandals and I am ready in fifteen. No one has to wait for me, ever. I am always ready ahead of time. *For what,* I think, *ready for what?*

Of course, Kai will be late. He always is, not a go-getter like I am. I guess opposites attract. He is so laid-back. No one down South has any sense of time. They are in no rush except in that darn traffic! The fast lane always runs as fast as it can. You would think it was the Autobahn. Not much controlling it either, it just keeps getting faster.

Atlanta used to be a sleepy city until all those Yankees came down and spoiled things. Now it is as fast-paced as New York City or Chicago. I have never been to those cities, but they cannot be as polite in traffic as people are here. It must be that entire "yes, ma'am," and "no, ma'am" thing. Their mamas raised them right.

"Hi, darlin'" Kai announces himself. "Y'all look good enough to eat! I'm a-fixin' to take you some place cool. Got a mind of where y'all want to head?"

I am not a southern belle as you may have suspected by now, all this southern lingo is making me smile. Somehow coming from this tall, lean, drink-of-water, as we say out West, it seems just right.

"Well, babe," say I, "let's go somewhere we can talk and cool off. How 'bout some Mexican?"

We mosey over to his old pickup, dark green, rusting and unwashed. The door creaks as he opens it for me. (Notice I am still in my Western mode, and *mosey* seems the right term to me. Maybe southerners do not mosey, I don't know.) At least he is a southern gentleman, which impresses me as much as his good looks. I wonder how he would do out in Wyoming where my dad put me on a horse before I could walk. At least this old pickup truck would fit right in.

Visions of my childhood linger in my mind, and I am back there in Cheyenne. My dad is holding the reins of the old Appaloosa, leading the mare with me on the back. "Hold on to the feathers" as I called the mane. *It is funny how I will always think of them as feathers.*

Mom was there for me too, but always in the background. She named me Elena, which Dad thought was a strange name for such an Irish-looking girl. He thought I should be Colleen or Mary, but Mom, being stubborn, named me Elena Marie Kelly.

As I grew older and was able to handle the mare by myself, Daddy was still there waiting for me. Bareback and barefoot, I rode like a young Indian. My knees gripped the sides of that old mare as the breeze whipped my long hair out behind me like a flame.

With the sun beating down on me, I hid under my old straw hat and begged, "When I gonna get some cowboy boots, Daddy? My feet are getting' sunburned."

"Soon as I get to town, baby, maybe next week."

His hands were creased and calloused as he gently lifted me down. I felt warm and loved as he held me, not realizing that his next trip to town would be his last. His old pickup truck, very much like the one we are riding in, would roll down the mountainside as it missed a sharp curve and burst into flame. My mom and daddy never made it out. My life changed forever.

I was seven years old and an orphan! How could I understand where heaven is? Why couldn't I go there too? No one would ever love me. No one would hold me gently as Daddy did.

The welfare worker was all business as she dragged me along crying and screaming, "I want my daddy!"

"Hush, child, someone will take care of you. I sure wish you had a relative somewhere, so I wouldn't have to go to all this trouble." So there I was—just trouble. A trouble someone would have to take care of. No one wanted trouble.

I cried for several days until Bob Craemer, a tall thin rancher from Butte, picked me up from Welfare Services. He was an ugly man made uglier by the scowl that he wore on his face continually. "I came to get ya," he scolded, "So don't give me no trouble!" I looked up in wonder at his weather-beaten face. I was trouble all right, no need to remind me, trouble and stubborn too. I would show them!

The scowl on his face scared me into obedience. Dragging my feet, I followed, wiping my runny nose with the sleeve of my shirt. We rode in silence in an old wood-paneled station wagon. The seats were worn and dusty. Miles went by as I dozed and woke with a start as we pulled into a yard full of tumbleweeds. "Git out, young'n, we're here." My unruly flame-red hair hid my face. The tears I had shed went unnoticed under the dust and grime that covered me.

The screen door slammed behind me as I shuffled into the log cabin. Bob's wife Jenny was thin with stringy hair. She was dressed in a worn dress that was several sizes too large and hung on her slender frame. Jenny looked at me sadly and said, "Don't pay him any mind. You are safe here. We will have plenty to eat, now that we've got you. The cabin is warm, and you can sleep up there in the loft."

I was too scared to cry, but I would not eat for my new foster parents, not that day anyway. I missed my daddy, and that gruff voice and scowl on Bob's face had me petrified. I was their meal ticket and nothing more.

There was no love there. It was a cold place, and I shiver at the thought.

Kai opens the door for me, and I return to the present. "What's up, babe, you cold? I noticed you shivering. You have not said a word since I picked you up. You mad or something?"

"No, just lost in thought."

"Good ones, I hope," he says as he looked at me sideways as though he is certain I am upset about something.

I guess he is probably right, but I do not want to tell him just yet about what I have decided. I know he will be disappointed, but I really do not want to leave Atlanta. It is the first place that I have felt good about myself.

This city terrifies me sometimes, but most of the time, it is home. The thrill of the fast lane, the parties, the Fox Theater, the perception that the city is alive makes me aware that this is where I belong. People are doing things here in Atlanta. I feel as though my life has some importance to it, a feeling I never had until I moved here. I do not want to lose it.

"Honey, would you like to order?" Kai asks as I sit, staring blindly at the menu.

"Surprise me. I'll have what you're having," I reply. That gets me off the hook. I really need to get myself back to the present. I will give him my full attention. If I only knew how to break the news to him gently, but all that can wait until we have finished the meal.

Kai reaches across the table and holds my hand in his. I feel the heat of his hand, and my heart skips a beat. "Just think, you and I can be together as a family. We can eat at home, and you can cook for me."

Now what can I say to that. I ignore the remark and change the subject. "I've heard the food here is really good. I'm not certain my cooking measures up," I protest.

"You cook it, I'll eat it."

"Don't make promises you can't keep," I tease. Cooking is not one of my greater accomplishments.

Kai's eyes are dark and mysterious, and his smile is infectious as I gaze at his face, trying to come up with the right words to express my sincere belief that I should remain in Atlanta. My resolve is starting to melt along with my heart. *Oh, why can't life be simple?* The food comes on steaming plates, and as much as I pay attention to it, it might as well be cold. I eat a bite and stir with my fork, dreading what I am about to say.

My reluctance to speak my mind spoils the mood. We both know that we have to discuss his proposal. Kai waits with anticipation for me to speak. I notice that he has not eaten much either. I really dread what I have to say.

All right, I guess I may as well tell him. "I love you, Kai, but I really have not thought about getting married just yet. It is just too soon."

"Do you have someone else? Or is it just me," he worries.

"I just like the status quo. I love Atlanta. I love my independence." There, now, he knows. *Well, that did not take long.* After all this worrying about how to tell him, it was such a simple statement.

"I'm not taking *no* for an answer, so what do I have to do to get you to come with me?"

He really does *not* get it. I guess I can think about it in a few more days.

Outside now, we walk slowly along, each of us lost in thought. There is a chill in the air. As I shiver, Kai reaches for me and presses his hard body against mine. His gentle lips against my neck are nibbling at my ear. Even in heels, I am much shorter than he is, but the size difference seems just right as we snuggle together as we have so many times before. The chill has disappeared with the heat wave his touch produces.

"Let's go to my place," Kai pleads as he opens the truck door for me, hoping that I cannot resist his invitation.

Just this one time, I rationalize, will not hurt, and we can say our good-byes at the end of next week when he leaves. As we step into his apartment, the phone is ringing. Kai ignores it. He is intent on pulling me along with him to his bedroom. He has only one thought on his mind, I realize, and I do not resist.

As he pulls his belt with a snap from his pants, I cringe, remembering the beating I used to get at the hands of that angry man at the first foster home when I was only seven. Maybe I deserved it. But what can a child of seven do to deserve being beaten with a belt? Time has blurred even the pain. My memory is only of that ugly man and his belt.

I shiver again as Kai pulls his sweater over his head. His musky smell fills me as I come to him. Our clothes are soon off, and our bodies pressed together in a familiar way.

Tonight is different somehow. Kai takes his time as we lay together touching, marveling at the wonder of each other. Passion is slowly rising as we become lost in the moment. We are two, then we are just one, joined together, one body, one soul, rising and falling as the tide. Hard bodies and soft places! Now I have someone with gentle hands to hold me as a vision of my daddy whispers, "Take love where you find it."

As if in response, Kai murmurs, "Elena, I love you. I do not want to lose you. You are mine and I am yours if you want me. Please marry me, Elena, and come with me. I know how hard it is for you to leave Atlanta, but we will find a way. I promise you!"

My response is automatic. How can I say no to this man? He is everything a woman could want—he is gentle and loving, and he treats me as though I were made of spun gold.

"I love you too, Kai. I will go with you," I reply, surprised at myself as I seal my fate. No regrets, at least not yet. Just as a flame attracts a moth and devours it, so Kai's embrace consummates my love for this man.

Sleep comes on angel wings as we hold each other, our lives and bodies entwined in peace. Yes, heaven is surely here.

Smyrna
Saturday morning
Kai

Now that I have Elena thinking my way, I cannot risk the possibility that she will change her mind. I know how set she is on Atlanta. This job is important too. Once I get started with the State, I should have endless possibilities, at least that is what they said when I put in my application. We need to get married right away, so we will have a place to live on the reservation.

Granny always said marriage was the only way to happiness. Elena and I have known each other long enough. We seem to get along, so I can see no reason not to get married. No long engagements, I feel we have already passed that stage. No living together without a commitment.

A baby would complete our lives. A little boy I can teach in the ways of my ancestors, the Native American way. A little girl would be a companion for Elena. I hope Elena feels the same way. All those foster homes that she experienced, Elena must have come away with regrets. She had no one who really cared for her. She must know how important a real family is. I grew up without my mom and essentially without a father. At least I had Granny and Tenika who loved me.

I wonder if Mina is still alive, and if she ever thinks of Tanika and me. If only I could find her. I have been looking all my life. I just do not know where to look. Now that both Granny and her sister are dead, Tanika is my only family.

Oh, Mina, where are you? Could Grandpa Willow Tree have been wrong?

Smyrna
Saturday morning
Elena

Waking up in an unfamiliar bed and only a dent where Kai was lying, I wonder what I am doing here. Where is here? Coffee is perking somewhere as I arise nude and confused. I find Kai's robe in the bathroom, wrap it around my slender body and run my fingers though my mop of curly hair.

Wishing I had my toothbrush, I splash water over my face with my hand and stare into the mirror. *So much for that!*

Kai is whistling in the kitchenette. Bacon is sizzling in the skillet, and I hear the toaster pop up. As he hears me, he calls, "Come here, darlin' breakfast is ready."

"I thought I was supposed to do the cooking for you," I call as I come around the corner. It sure smells good, and I really am hungry this morning. "Last night was the best, hon. When you leave next Friday, will you be going to train at Forsyth?"

"Yeah, sugar, I will have to be gone a month. We can get married before I go. Can we get the blood test on Monday?" he asks as he sits, smiling at me across the table. "It takes three days, so we can get married on Thursday before I leave. The justice of the peace over in Marietta should do the trick."

"Whoa, partner, what's the rush? A girl needs some time to plan a wedding!" *Did I really break my promise to myself to stay here in Atlanta?* Sometimes I get carried away with the moment. I am not so sure this morning that leaving Atlanta is what I want to do.

"Sugar, I just don't want to wait. Y'all might change your mind. You said you would last night, but I know how women change their minds."

This is my chance to tell him that yes, I have changed my mind, but I kept silent. I cannot stand to break his heart as he so tenderly looks at me. *Maybe we can make it.* He seems so sure.

"All right, honey, you name the time and place and I'll take you up on that. Do I at least, get a ring?" I tease. "But right now I just want to eat."

That settled we eat in silence. My mind is racing at the thought of leaving my job, Atlanta and poor old Cyclops. I wonder who will take my place there. I have to check my lease, tell my boss and get ready to move all in four weeks. There is so much to do, but I can get it done. It will just take some organized planning. No problem! I have always been an organized person. Now is the time to put it to the ultimate test.

I am still not certain why I consented to this marriage, but it seems fate would have it so. If not fate, why has my job ended right at this crucial time? Everything has fallen into place against my better judgment. My entire philosophy has changed in just a stolen moment.

I am not certain I am ready to leave my comfort zone for the unknown. Atlanta has been a security blanket for me. Irv is the anchor that keeps me grounded here in this city. He has been my substitute father, my mentor, and my confidant. I will miss him more than the city itself. For a girl that pretends to be self-sufficient, I certainly feel lost. I must not be as sure of myself as I thought.

Time is getting short if I am going to change my mind. At least I have this weekend.

Chapter 7

MINA'S QUEST

Seymour Johnson Air Force Base, North Carolina
1983
Mina

It is wonderful to be in the South again after all these years. I cannot remember being this warm in a long time. It is funny how coming back stirs up all the memories. I feel like a young girl again here although I am definitely not. Do we ever feel old in our minds? I still picture myself as young, so that I am startled to look in the mirror and see that aging face. When I look at myself, I see my mother.

This is a much larger base than the other two. It has a history of being one of the two fighter units to trace its history to another country. Before the entry of the United States into the Second World War, American volunteers were already serving in the Royal Air Force in Britain. When America entered the war, these units and the airmen were transferred here and became the Fourth Fighter Group in 1942. Their motto is Fourth but First.

Mark is very glad to serve with this fighter group. He is servicing the converted ARN-101-equiped aircraft that is planning to conduct experiments with the GBU-15 guided bomb units.

I am not certain what this means, but I listen to the men talk. My experience was with transports and bombers. I have no experience with these faster fighters and their ordinance.

This is a very proud unit according to Mark. He feels that it will be a force to reckon with in the days to come. The guided bombs should make target acquisition and accuracy more precise.

Mark and I make a trip out to the old homeplace in Swannanoa. The trip out here is long, but worth it for me, even though everything is deserted. The tumbledown shack we lived in is still here. The roof has caved in, and the front door is off. Over beside the creek, we find Grandpa Willow Tree, his gnarled roots sticking out of the bank into the water. He is not the way I remember him although his roots are even larger, and he is still clinging to life.

I knew something must have happened to Mama. She was so old when I was born, and we had not found a trace of her in Missouri where the report showed she had moved. She was the youngest of her family. I am certain her older sister is gone also. I did not know her grave was here. A simple stone marks her grave. I read the inscription, kneel down and weep:

Niabi Harjo
1893-1981
Beloved mother and grandmother

"Mama, forgive me, I was not the daughter you wanted. I loved you, but I did not know how to show it. If I could do it over, I would. We just do not get a second time around. Mama, I hope you are proud of me now. I have been a good mother to my second family, and I am searching desperately for my other children. If you can, help me find them. I love you, Mama. I hope you can hear my prayer."

They buried her here in the shelter of that old tree. This must please her spirit, as she loved this old Grandpa Willow. She spent almost a lifetime living in his shadow. I was surprised to find that old tree still alive.

Beside Niabi is an older marker. This one is very difficult to read as the sandstone has eroded. I take a piece of paper and a pencil and make a rubbing of the simple inscription.

Flight Harjo
1880-1956

"I remember you very well, Daddy, forgive me for not coming here sooner. Mama was strict, and I was stubborn. You were the one who was always there for me. You made excuses for my behavior, saying, 'Leave her alone, she is just showing her tail. Mina will grow up soon enough. Just let her be.' You would pick me up and hug me.

I loved you, Daddy, I am sorry I was such a stubborn girl. My heart is breaking now. Things could have been so different, if I had just listened to Mama."

I am still crying as I pour out my grief to the old willow. Sitting beneath its branches as Mama had, I asked, "Old Grandpa Willow Tree, help me find my children."

Mark laughs at me for talking to that old wizened tree. He may laugh, but it makes me feel better. Reverently, I take some cuttings from some of his better branches. I will plant them in my yard. Maybe they will grow if I tend to them. They are all I have of the past.

"Good-bye, Grandpa," I whisper as we leave, grasping his branches firmly in my hand.

Back at the base, Flight is upset because the air force moved us, and he is raising a fuss. He does not want new friends. He liked the old ones. He just turned four, which is a little early to form lasting friendships. As soon as he meets the local children, Flight will come around. The base here is in a safe area and is one of the leading bases in the county.

I wish we were in the mountains, but I will settle for just being in the South. We may have to wait until Mark retires, but my dream is to live again in the Carolina hill country with Mark.

Mark does not know it yet, but I am pregnant. I am going to surprise him this evening. He just loves children. This will probably be our last child if I can carry it to term. My season for children is just about over although Mama had me when she was older still. I really would like another boy, so Flight can have a playmate.

I hired a detective, Bob Frasier, when I first got here. Bob came back with a report that my family had left this place and gone to Missouri. When he tried to trace them there, no one had heard of them. It has been too long ago. All of the relatives were old when mother went there.

Tanika must be married by now, so she will have a new name. Kai should be easier to find. Mark suggested we search the records for the armed services. "If Kai was ever in the service, we may be able to find him." We sent the detective back to try to trace government records. It is just a long shot, but we do not know any place else to start. Anything is worth a try.

Chapter 8

JINXED

Smyrna
Sunday morning
Kai

I hope all this works out. It seems as though I have a jinx as far as making things work out. Elena said yes—that is the important thing. I was so afraid that she would refuse.

I do not know what's in my savings account, but I am going to get her the best damn ring money can buy—at least, my money. Elena's eyes are green. I want an emerald to match her beautiful eyes, but of course, she will want a diamond, so I would like to find a ring with both.

Shopping is more important today than Jerome's roof. It is just about finished anyway. I am fixin' to get Tanika to go with me. She has such good taste, and I hate shopping.

After looking in several stores, I am amazed at how many different rings are available. Most of them are very expensive. Of course, Tanika has taken me to all the exclusive shops. She seems to know where they are all located. She must do a lot of shopping.

We spend a good bit of the day looking. Most of the rings are just diamonds. Some even have rubies and diamonds or just emeralds. Most of them are very expensive. I am beginning to think I will have to settle for something else.

Finally, Tanika has a ring spotted. Elena will love it. I will find out what size she wears. It is going to be more money than I thought, but all the rest of the rings just do not compare. The jeweler says he will size it to fit, and he will hold it for me. I put a down payment on the ring with what is in my billfold. When we go get our blood tests, I will get the money from savings. I cannot wait to show this ring to Elena. I will give it to her tomorrow night. We can have it sized before the wedding.

Now I must finish that roof! How I hate this job, but it has to be finished. I feel more obligated than ever to get it completed, if not for Jerome at least for Tenika.

North Cobb
Monday morning
Elena

How organized I have become and self-reliant, unlike that pathetic know-nothing girl I was before Atlanta. Two and a half years have made all the difference. As a caterpillar emerging from a cocoon and turning into a butterfly, I have emerged triumphant. My pride may be my Achilles' heel along with my willful nature.

When Irv took me in and taught me, I had never worked in an office. In fact, I had never done anything but wait tables or work at petty jobs that paid minimum wage. Irv brought me into the workforce. He taught me how to dress, how to type, and how to process words on a computer. He gave me the confidence to go out to work in the city.

At first, I spent many hours on roads I did not know in traffic I did not understand. Gradually, I became a part of this Atlanta, this sprawling traffic jam down South. The year was 1981, and computers were just coming of age.

Word processors were huge raw machines that sometimes did what you asked of them if you knew the right language.

Now three years later, I am doing my thing, working for my living. Computers are becoming more commonplace. I will bet someday everyone will have one. Secretaries will use them, and the dinosaurs I use will be obsolete. Maybe I will be too. I am lost in thought over that.

Efficiency is crucial as I make a mental note to accomplish as much as I can. I arrange for the blood test. Kai and I meet at noon and go to the clinic where we both end up with Band-Aids on our arms.

I call Irv and tell him I am moving and no longer available.

He says, "Oh, by the way, I meant to tell you that your job will be over next week. I will miss you. I had another assignment lined up for you, but if you are going to be gone, I will give it to Jillian. Good luck, Elena." Irv sounds relieved that he will not have to find a job for both of us.

We really have to stretch my money. I have a paid-up credit card for $1,000. I will let Kai have it. I know he does not have one, and he will need money more than I will for Forsyth.

If I only get one more paycheck, I am going to be short two weeks' worth. Well, I can handle that, I guess. I will check my savings account as small as it is, not eat out and have a yard sale on Saturday. Maybe on two Saturdays, I am such a pack rat and have so much stuff. I can move more efficiently with less of that junk to move.

Next, I call the real estate agent to see about my lease. This works out pretty well as I had forgotten to renew in February, so I am just renting month to month. *I wonder how that slipped my mind.* I give him a month's notice. We should be gone before this month is up.

That just leaves getting married, planning the yard sales and packing to move. Oh yes, and renting a U-haul! I will need a big truck and have to tow my little red bug.

Sandy Plains
He discovers Elena is getting married.
Irv

I have been in love with Elena since she first came to me. She has never looked on me as anything but an employer. It is my fault. I knew I was a little too old for her, and so I never let her know that I cared for her in anything but a professional way. My heart feels as though it is going to break now that she is leaving. No one else can ever take Elena's place. I know I should be happy that she has found her true love. She sounded so excited when she called. Elena said she would stop by before she left. I will try not to let on how much I care.

North Carolina
February 1984
Mina

Yeah! Bob our detective found that Kai had been in the marines. His forwarding address was Missouri, but he is not there now. He must have planned to go back with Mother there. We searched through the motor vehicle registrations in Missouri. No license issued to any Harjo. Bob has not given up hope however. He is searching for registrations in some of the surrounding states. We think Kai would want to remain in the South. It may take some time, but we will find him.

Mark and I have a new baby girl. We named her Regina, after Mark's mother and Fawn (Niabi) after mine: Regina Fawn Foster. I know Mother would not object to the translation of her name as Fawn. It is more in keeping with modern times. Mark and I have decided, now we have both a boy and a girl, that our family is complete. It would be, of course, more complete if we could find Kai and Tanika.

Four children: two grown and two little ones, I have really been blessed.

Two of my willow cuttings did grow. I have kept them watered well and in full sun here at the airbase. They have grown as tall as Mark, but I have not yet tried to have a "conversation" with the trees as Mark calls it. He is a nonbeliever in the magic of the willow. Old traditions are lost on Mark. Unless he can prove it, he does not believe it. It must be his scientific mind.

Flight has made many new friends here in kindergarten. He is not only popular but also very intelligent. He is already reading at a third-grade level and he is a wiz at math.

We would like to stay in North Carolina although you never know when or if they will move us. Mark says, "We go where they send us. Wherever the air force has a base, I am willing to go. Serving my country is all that I have ever wanted to do. Of course, having a family comes first." (He knew he had better add the part about the family.)

Atlanta
1984, Tuesday afternoon
Elena

Here I am again in rush-hour traffic, driving home. Tuesday is even warmer than last Friday. I have so much on my mind that it is hard to concentrate in this heat and traffic while planning my life at the same time. I pride myself on efficiency, but I have about reached my limit—too much to do and too little time.

Leaving Atlanta is the last thing I want to do, but leaving this traffic behind, oh *yes,* I can do that.

Rush hour seems to be worse today than usual. I cannot seem to get into the lane I would like. Too many cars are going too fast, and a wreck with two police cars in the outside lane is pulling all the traffic over making all cars and semis pull into the next lane.

Distracted by the change in the traffic pattern, I do not see the blue van in the next lane until it actually crashes into me carrying my Volkswagen into the center wall of I-285. I fight to correct my path, but the much-heavier van takes me with it. It is a frightening feeling to lose complete control of my direction.

Hitting my brakes has very little effect as I scrape along the wall. It is happening so rapidly that I have no time to think. Centrifugal force is forcing my body toward the steering column as I brace my hands ineffectively against the wheel. The forward movement of the two cars stops, but my head does not, carrying my forehead into the rearview mirror as the world fades to gray.

When I open my eyes, again the world is white, very white and bright. Antiseptic smells assail my nose, my head hurts, and I feel woozy. It must be a strange dream and I need to go back to sleep. My eyes close again but I hear voices. They seem to be so far away.

"Poor dear, she hasn't come to yet!"

Streaks behind my eyelids, a buzzing sound and a feeling of rocking back and forth confuses me. My left arm feels cold. My right knee is throbbing. It is hard to breathe. *Do I have a hat on?* This is some strange dream! Someone is calling my name,

"Elena, can you hear me?"

Yes, I think I do.

Are you someone in my dream? With effort, I open my eyes again. This white person seems as if she is a hologram against a sparkling white background.

"Oh, Elena, good you are awake."

The room starts to come into focus and the hologram is a nurse in white scrubs. She is holding my right arm applying a blood pressure cuff. "You had us worried, you have been asleep for so long. How do you feel?"

My lips are dry and cracked, and my tongue sticks to the roof of my mouth as I try to answer. "Water," I gasp.

The nurse puts some ice chips on my tongue. "No water yet, just a little ice."

I cannot remember how I got here or what day it is. I am so sleepy that I nod off again. Dreams come and go. I am on a ship, and the ocean is rocking the boat back and forth. I am constantly waking up and falling back to sleep. I have called the nurse several times, only to get more ice chips and my lips sponged off. Although I know I am hurt, I do not remember how I got here or what day it is.

Smyrna
Tuesday afternoon
Kai

Hey, things are working out for Elena and me. I was afraid there for a while that she would change her mind. She looked so uncertain. She must be serious now after taking that blood test. I wonder why she does not answer her phone. Maybe I will just run over there and wait for her. She should have been back from work by now.

The ring I bought took almost all my savings, but she is worth it. I could not resist the emerald. It just matches her eyes. She had better like it. It is hard for a man to know what a woman would like. I really want to surprise her.

Driving over to North Cobb in front of her pretty house, I can see why she does not want to leave it. The roses are just starting to bloom. But where is she? Her car is not here. *She has to come home some time, so I will just sit here and wait.* I am glad I have that key she gave me to feed her cat. It is too hot to wait in the truck.

Time drags while you are waiting for someone. I open a can of food for the cat. She rubs up to my leg, then gets busy, and chows down. *How cats can eat that stuff, it smells awful!*

I call Corporate Headquarters. I get the recording. Maybe Elena stopped somewhere. I thought she was coming straight home. When I talked to her at noon, she told me she would be home right after work.

There is no choice now. It is Wednesday, 10:00 AM. I must have fallen asleep. I waited up all night. *Here is the phone book, yeah here it is—highway patrol.*

"My girlfriend Elena Kelley is driving a red Volkswagen. No, I do not have the tag number, but she never arrived home. Will you call me back if you hear anything? Yeah—at this number. Thanks, I'll wait here."

No one is calling back and I am frantic, but I stay riveted to the spot, so I can answer the phone.

Finally, after three hours, the phone rings. "Accident—Oh no! Do you know where they took her? No. OK. I'll check the hospitals." I am shaking so badly I can hardly read the phone book.

Everywhere I phone, I get a "not here": Not at Kennestone, no record at Northside Hospital, where do you suppose they took her? Oh yeah, probably Grady.

"Hello, I am searching for Elena Kelly. No, she does not work there. They brought her in as an emergency. Will you check please? Did you say *no information unless I am a relative?* This is her husband, is she badly hurt?"

"Is she in Intensive care? Will I be able to see her? I'll be right there."

I am not her husband yet, but a little white lie will not hurt. Hurrying now, I jump in my truck, skid around the corner and head downtown for Grady Hospital. It takes me awhile to find a parking space, so I rush up to the visitor's desk on the dead run.

The receptionist stares at me as I ask about Elena. She is in intensive care, two floors up and on the left side. *How well can she be if she is intensive care?* Those two words strike terror in my heart.

The receptionist can see how nervous I am and decides to show me the way herself. As we walk along, I am praying. *Oh, please, Lord, let her be all right.*

Oh, why did this have to happen just as things were working out for us? We had it all planned. We were to get married. Elena, I love you so much. I just cannot believe it. The jinx is still here!

Grady Hospital
Wednesday afternoon
Elena

Someone is calling my name again, "Elena, Elena."

As I open my eyes again, trying to focus, a very worried-looking man is trying to get my attention. "I finally found you. When you weren't at home when I called I did not know where you had gone. I waited until morning, and you still weren't there. I finally called the police to say you were missing. Someone called me back this afternoon and reported you had been in an accident. I called all the hospitals and finally found you here at Grady. I had to tell them you were my wife in order to see you."

My mind cannot seem to register that, and I smile and doze off. Time is warped either asleep or awake. I hear those buzzing sounds again, and I am still floating in space. Nurses keep coming and going.

Pain returns as I begin to wake up. It is dark when I open my eyes again.

"Did that ship I was on sink? How did I get here?" After that strange query, thoughts start to make a little more sense.

I was just dreaming. I remember a man. Do I have a husband? Did I dream someone was here, someone who cared?

My headache is getting worse, and I reach up with my free right hand to find my bandaged forehead along with tape on my nose. I discover tubes attached to my left arm. The constant drip of the saline solution is making my arm cold. I am shivering. A cast encases my right leg. Feeling around again, I find the call button.

The overhead light goes on.

"Good, you are awake," says this cheery voice. "It's just about morning, how about some water?"

Water at last! She lets me have a couple of sips and I start to feel a little more human.

"We will be moving you into a regular room in just a few minutes. You're in ICU, but now you are awake I think you will find a room more comfortable."

80

"Thanks," I managed to say. "Could I get another blanket?"

"Sure thing, sweet, coming right up!"

The blanket she brings is warm. *Happiness is a warm blanket,* I think as I fall asleep again. My bed is moving and I hear the elevator, but snooze right through the journey to my room.

Morning brings the dozing hospital to life at five-thirty. When the room lights turn on, I find I have a roommate. She is snoring away, oblivious to the light, the noise and the commotion. My eyes are wide-open now. All the usual embarrassing things are about to take place. My curtain is drawn. The bedpan is cold as ice. Who chills those things? My draw sheet is changed which rattles me around and makes my head hurt. In fact, everything hurts.

If you have ever been in a hospital, you know the routine. By the time the wrecking crew is done, I am sitting in a chair. My leg must weigh as much as I do. It is propped on a stool. I am dizzy sitting here, but it is much better than lying on my sore back.

No one has ever answered my question, how did I get here? I have so many questions, what about work, what day is it, what do I do now, where is the doctor, when can I go home and most of all, what happened to Kai?

All those thousand of thoughts in my unclear mind keep bouncing around as if they are ping-pong balls. No wonder my head hurts.

What is under these bandages anyway? I have not seen myself in a mirror, but just feeling around I know I am swollen, bandaged and probably stitched. I think I can feel the stitches pulling. I really would like something for pain.

The nurse says, "Sorry, head injury, no pain pill, we need to wait until we see the doctor. It's time to put you back to bed."

Hopping on one foot, I reach the bed and slide under the cool sheets. That transition went fairly well. I am just happy to lie down.

Just as they bring in a meal tray (food at last), a young man, telling me he is Dr. Farquart, asks the usual questions: How was your night? Did you sleep? Have you been up yet? I have a thermometer in my mouth so an answer is impossible. He shines a light in my eyes, takes my pulse and seems satisfied with what he sees, mumbles something to the nurse and leaves before I can think of one question to ask him.

That went well, I do not know anymore than I did!

The breakfast that has been cooling is the usual hospital fare: Jell-O, broth, apple juice, tea, nothing of substance just enough to make me think I am starving. The Jell-O is warm and melting. The apple juice is warm. The broth is cold. The only thing warm enough is the tea, which I drink and leave the rest.

Flowers arrive, tulips, in every shade imaginable and behind the flowers, Kai appears with a silly grin on his face.

"I thought y'all needed to brighten up this room a bit. When are we getting married or have you changed your mind already. I have that ring you wanted. I measured your finger while you were sleeping."

"How can you think of marriage at a time like this? I cannot walk and heaven only knows what I look like under all these bandages. You may not even want to marry me when you look at all the scars.

"Do you know what happened to me, what happened to my little red bug, where did they take it, what about my job, and who has my cat?"

"Darlin', you know I can't answer all that. I have your cat. Who cares about the car? I understand it is a total wreck. They had to pry you out of it. Yes, I do want to marry you, scars and all. You have to quit your job anyway because you are coming with me.

"I have all your stuff packed. I reserved a house and as soon as we get this marriage thing over with, and you are out of here, I'll get a U-Haul, tow my truck and we're off."

"Well, Mr. Take-Charge, I guess you have it all planned." I am looking at him with my bandaged face bewildered by his determined look. "So who's going to do the honors of marrying us?"

"I've got that all lined up too. He is coming tomorrow."

"Where, here? It cannot be. No one gets married in a hospital room. This is just too much."

"Nope, you'll see. My sister will stop by this afternoon. She has it all worked out. Just wait until she gets here with her surprise."

His sister has never had a thing to do with me. I only met her once. All I can remember is that she is very tall, dark and aloof. I cannot remember what she does for a living. What can be her surprise?

I have a headache now, big time. "OK, honey, I'll just have to trust you. What else can I do just lying here anyway?" How my life has gone downhill, I cannot even plan my own wedding. I cannot even get up by myself. I have this ton of plaster on my leg and those darn tubes attached everywhere. Maybe I can wear this bare-bottomed sissy-printed hospital gown for my wedding.

"Just kiss me and leave."

Kai is still wearing that silly grin as he leans down and plants a wet kiss on my cheek. "Tomorrow will be terrific, you just wait and see. I guarantee it will be unique.

"Let me try this ring on your finger." He kisses my fingers and holds my hand up for me. "Do you like it? I searched all over for the right one. It seems to fit."

"Oh! It's beautiful!" Emerald and diamonds in a cluster twinkle on my finger. I forget my headache, my bandaged head and my nose as I pull Kai down for a real kiss. My tulips on the nightstand seem to nod in agreement. I am tired from the morning's activities and as I yawn, Kai slips away without another word.

Smyrna
Thursday
Kai

So many promises, I hope we can pull this thing off. Things never seem to work out for me. If I live to be one hundred, I will never understand why God lets bad things happen to good people. At least, I think I am a good person. I know Elena is.

My sister thinks she can do anything. I sure hope she is right. This is going to be the most important day of our lives, and I do not want anything to spoil it.

Chapter 9

THE WEDDING

Damn, Elena looks rough. I just could not tell her how badly she is hurt. Got to get back and get this all done. I cannot let Elena change her mind. She did not even recognize me the first day. I was afraid she had amnesia. Her head is so beat-up. No wonder she is confused. I love her. I do not care what she looks like. I just want her to be with me. It is hard to concentrate on anything. I just have so much to do.

This deadline for work is approaching, and I need that job. I am so sick of working for my sister especially for her husband, Jerome. He thinks I owe him the world.

If I can give the roof my full attention for the next two hours, I will have it finished—*if I can give anything my full attention.*

Grady Hospital
Thursday afternoon
Elena

I doze off for a few minutes. A nurse awakens me. "You have a visitor, but first I shall remove these tubes from your arm. You do not need them now that you are drinking fluid. Doctor has ordered a pain pill, so let's take that first. Later, we are going for a walk in the hall."

Free at last, I glance over at the ring. *Kai must have spent everything he has on this thing.* It is beautiful, but how did he afford it? He never seems to have any money. We have nothing saved for this marriage. Guess we will just have to live on love!

Kai's sister, in a canary yellow A-line dress, rushes in. That yellow really sets off her dark skin. She is much darker than Kai. "Hi, Tanika," I remark (glad that I remember her name).

"Oh, Elena, so glad you are awake, I have been waiting to see you. I have been shopping. Hope you like everything. Kai told me you had a bandage on your head, so I brought this tiara and veil. Let's see—yes, it will cover nicely. I will hang your dress in your closet. You are a size 6, right?"

She shows me a beautiful gown, ivory, strapless, with built-in bra. "The long full skirt will cover your cast, and I bought a satin cover for the wheelchair, 'cause I know you can't walk. The minister will be here tomorrow at one-thirty. We have the chapel here in the hospital reserved, and I will have it decorated, of course. The hospital says we can use the lunchroom for the cake and the guests."

I am crying now, thinking I do not have anyone to invite. "How will I ever thank you?" I sob.

"Just take good care of my baby brother. He has been so upset that you were hurt, and he cannot wait to get married. I don't really know you, but he thinks you are the greatest so don't let him down." She gives me a disapproving look as if she just knows that I will be a disappointment.

Smyrna
Day before the wedding
Kai

Now the day is almost here, I am so nervous. Guess all new bridegrooms are nervous. I polish my black shoes so shiny even the Marine Corps would approve. Elena cannot back out now.

I think I have everything ready for the move. Everything is packed and ready to go. I hope Elena will be ready to leave the hospital in time. It is going to be a rough trip for her in her condition.

Let's see, got my tuxedo, thanks to Tanika. The roof is finished. Jerome is satisfied—that is really a first. How Tanika puts up with him I do not know. Jerome is a jerk in my book, but he is family, and Tanika loves him, so that is all that matters.

Tanika just found out she is pregnant. I hope Elena and I will not have to wait as long as they have for a baby. Jerome and Tanika have been trying for three years. I am so happy for her.

Tanika has been so wonderful about this wedding. She did all the arrangements. She insisted on paying for everything, even the dress, the cake and the flowers. My only expense was that ring. It is beautiful, but so expensive.

Everything is all set. Elena and I will be husband and wife tomorrow.

Mina, I hope you will be happy for us wherever you are. Grandpa Willow Tree, if you are still out there, please give us your blessing.

Grady Hospital
Friday morning
Elena

Tomorrow is here already. I have had the tape removed from my nose, and I have smudged makeup over the scab. At least there are no stitches there. Makeup and all, my nose is so swollen that it is a good thing I have the veil. We fluff up my hair the best we can with this bandage over part of it and put on my dress, which is a little large. I have lost some weight in the hospital. I am barefoot and have a cast on my leg.

Tanika has loaned me an emerald pendant for something borrowed, and puts a blue garter on my good leg "for luck," she says. She arranges the tiara and veil. When the nurse brings the chair, Tanika drapes it with the satin coverlet and ties on a willow branch. *What is that branch for?* I wonder. I hobble over to the chair, and she spreads that full-skirted gown over all.

She looks at me with approval. "Not bad for a cripple!" Tanika teases as she puts a big bridal bouquet into my arms.

Jerome Tanika's husband has a camera and although I am not too fond of how I look, I will need these pictures to remember this unusual occasion. I do not know if a hospital wedding is a first or not, but it is a first and last for me.

A surprise comes in the form of Irv. "I'm here to give you away," he says with pride. "I also invited some of my regular temps, hope that is OK with you. I think you know most of them."

I have never seen Irv in a tuxedo. He is more handsome than I remembered. Irv takes control of the chair, and away we go to the chapel. Jerome takes a picture of Irv and me.

Tanika is leading the way, and nurses, all smiling, are opening doors as we come to them. Someone brought a guitar, and soft music accompanies us down the aisle.

Kai is standing there waiting for me in a tuxedo. I have never seen him before in anything but jeans. He is so good-looking. Kai looks much taller than his six foot seven inches. I wonder how they got tuxedo pants long enough for his long legs.

The justice of the peace is an elderly black man with curls that he has slicked down with what looks like a pound of grease. He has parted his black hair in the middle, and there is a white streak on each temple. He has a clear bass voice that echoes across the partially empty chapel.

With Irv declaring that he is the one giving me away, I feel all choked up and so thrilled I can hardly speak my lines. What ever happens from this day forward, this is worth it.

If only my daddy could see me now, but somehow I think, he is watching. I can feel his presence. I know he would approve of Kai. *I love him so much, Daddy.*

Smyrna
On his wedding night
Kai

I really cannot believe this! I have to leave my bride at the hospital until tomorrow so they can check her over before she leaves. They would not even let me stay the night with her, just sent me home. We have the rest of our lives, but it is a bummer to spend our wedding night alone.

It is probably for the best because I have to finish everything. Time is getting so short. I cannot leave Elena here because I have everything of hers packed and out of her house. I turned her key in to her landlord. If she is up to it, we will be leaving tomorrow.

I will try to make the trip as easy for her as possible, but it is a long way, and she may get too tired. Have to go to sleep now. I will need an early start. I really hate being alone tonight.

Chapter 10

OUT OF THE FAST LANE

On The Road
Saturday
Kai

It is raining. Actually, it has been raining nonstop for the last forty-eight hours. I remember reading some old map that identified Georgia as a "monsoon and rain forest." I am driving the U-Haul with the old truck in tow. Crossing the Chattahoochee, I cannot tell if we are on the highway or in the river. It is just as wet in both places. The wipers are scraping away at full speed, but the visibility is limited to the hood of the truck. We have some four hours to travel today. Elena's leg is still in the cast, the bandages are off her head, and the stitches are out. She has a bald spot and a very swollen nose.

Elena is acting like a spoiled brat that I am taking somewhere she does not want to go. Hell, I guess the best thing is just to leave her alone. Driving is taking all my attention anyway. I remember promising for better or worse, but so far, it seems to be worse. Not that I expect much because I know she is hurting, but she could at least talk or smile. This is supposed to be our honeymoon.

Large semis splash us with water as they pass and the wind is whipping us back and forth. Even the weather seems to be against this move.

Time passes slowly as the miles roll by until we eventually pull over for gas. We ask the attendant for directions. He is almost as wide as he is tall and wearing this huge pair of coveralls covered in oil and dirt. His hair is long and almost as dirty as his coveralls. He has a large wad of tobacco in his cheeks that reminds me of an overfed squirrel.

Dripping tobacco juice down his chin, he spits and wipes his mouth with the back of his tobacco-stained shirtsleeve and drawls, "Just get back on that road over yonder and haul ass!"

That breaks the somber mood as we get back on the road and *haul ass*. At least we are both smiling now, and the rain has let up. The rest of the trip will be easier now that Elena is talking to me again. I hope she will continue to be in a good mood. The driving is much easier now that I can see the highway, and I can pay more attention to her.

On the Road
Several hours later
Elena

I am dozing which helps with the boredom. Snatches of memory surface in my semi-comatose mind.

I am riding on the front of a bike. A woman is peddling. A large man is riding on the bike ahead. We stop and the man is selling the bikes to someone for a few dollars.

The woman pulls me along the sidewalk into some kind of grocery store. She buys a loaf of white bread. We walk down several streets eating the bread. Nothing is on the bread, but it tastes so good. I never knew bread could be this delicious. The large man spots two more bicycles leaning against a fence. He spends some time looking around. Seeing no one, he jumps onto one of the bikes and starts peddling.

The woman grabs the other bike. This one has a carrier on the back and a basket on the front. Quickly, we get on the bike, me on the carrier, and the woman on the front. I am holding on as we race through town.

I come back to the present, thinking he must have stolen those bikes. *Who were those people?* I wonder. Much of my past, I cannot remember. I do remember the wonderful taste of that bread. Awake now, I look out the window. It has started raining again.

Pain is starting to make me miserable again, and I find the pills I brought from the hospital pharmacy, find a bottle of water we have stashed and take two. I am trying my best not to complain. This trip is becoming a real hardship for mc so soon out of the hospital.

Kai reaches over and touches my hand, and contentment again fills my being. It is amazing how his hands comfort me.

Looking up, I smile at him and whisper, "I love you." Miles go by quickly now, or so it seems as our thought come together again as one.

The exit we need is just ahead. It is clearly marked, so Kai has no trouble finding it. It is beginning to rain again, but just enough that Kai has to use the wipers. They make a slapping sound on the semidry window.

Chapter 11

THE PRISON

The Prison
Friday afternoon
Kai

Good, I guess I was just imagining things. Elena must be hurting and not complaining. I need to be more sensitive to her feelings. They never taught us sensitivity in the marines, only discipline and hardship. I could have re-upped instead of taking a State job. Elena would have gone along with that, but we are stuck with my decision now for better or worse.

Small houses appear on the narrow road that winds through tobacco-drying sheds, farmland and a few cows. Most of the shacks along the way are unpainted. Some have trucks in the yards. Some of the trucks actually have wheels. Piles of cans and rusty old farm tractors are interspersed with rows of tobacco plants—row upon row of tobacco. The big leaves catch the raindrops and drip off.

The prison looms in the distance with coiled strands of razor wire. A tall chain-link fence topped with and surrounded by rows and rows of shiny wire makes the prison look very secure. It has towers like sentinels on each corner as well as a tower in the center of each quadrant.

Directly across the road is a smaller more modern building, which, I understand, is only a medium-security facility. Chain link fence and razor wire surround it as well.

Inmates do most of the farming from the smaller prison although work groups go out under guard from the big prison also. The prison farm produces almost all the food necessary to feed both institutions. I tell Elena this is the prison reservation, and we are lucky to have gotten a house on the farm here.

We turn off just before we get to the main gate of the prison and travel down a narrow mud road. This damn rain has made the area a big puddle of mud. Large puddles of water with ruts almost stop our forward progress as we bump along on the lane turning into an area of three small stucco houses with a drive up to each one.

There is not much grass, mostly wet sand and a couple of trees next to the houses, but no flowers or flowering bushes. There are just barren-looking small stucco houses that cannot have more than two bedrooms.

We have a lot of furniture with us in the large U-Haul. There is more than enough for at least two houses this size. I hope Elena is not too disappointed. Really, I had no idea it looked so barren, but then again, it can be fixed up. Convincing Elena may be difficult.

The Reservation
Arriving at the houses
Elena

As we turn into the drive for the first house, Kai is grinning and says, "Welcome home."

Opening the door, he scoops me up, wades through the mud and sand to deposit me in the living room. I gaze in horror at the scene. Dirt is everywhere—mud, paper debris and cobwebs.

Combined with the living room is the kitchen with painted cupboard doors hanging off their hinges. The kitchen area has something piled in the middle of the floor.

"Blood!

"Someone has butchered something in the middle of the kitchen!" I scream.

A snake crawls out of the laundry room next to the kitchen. It must have come in through the open hole for the dryer vent. Black flies are everywhere, buzzing around the blood pile. I feel as though I am going to faint.

Kai dispatches the snake with my crutches he brought in from the truck and throws the carcass out in the yard. He seems to have the situation under control, except for his screaming wife.

Someone left a peeling plastic chair in the middle of the floor, and I gladly plop down in it, ignoring the dirt.

"Welcome to hell is more like it," I moan.

Postponing the inevitable unloading of the U-Haul until this pouring rain stops, I hobble around the rest of this mansion on my crutches. Twin cots with iron frames and lumpy dirty mattresses are in the first bedroom.

The second bedroom is bare except for pieces of paper cut out from a catalog of women's underwear and bras and skimpy bathing suits, which are strewn all over the floor. "Sick," I hiss.

What we need is a shovel to scrape up this floor and a hose to hose it out—two things that we do not have with us. We cannot even bring in the furniture we brought until we clean up this mess.

I am tired, but not tired enough to lie down on those filthy mattresses. It is late in the afternoon. Kai, I know, is probably more tired than I am, but more cheerful.

"Let's go unhook my truck, and drive into town, he says, "We can find a place to stay, and we can tackle this in the morning. I do not have to report to work until Monday."

"Sounds like a plan!" I do not want to tell him how disappointed I am. I am not afraid of work, but this place looks hopeless.

We spend a few of our dwindling supply of dollars on a cheap motel not too far back up the way we came. It is great to stretch out in a bed. We snuggle together as close as we can get with this cast on my ankle. This is the first time we have had to make love since our wedding.

Not very romantic, but as I keep telling myself, we have the rest of our lives. The motel does not even have air-conditioning, but it has screens on the windows, and the night is cool from all that rain.

The sun, which has been hiding from us for days, sneaks up over the horizon as we stuff ourselves back into Kai's old truck, splashing through puddles on the way back to the reservation.

"Out of the fast lane, into the mud hole" I mutter although Kai is busy driving and unaware of my sarcasm. I really do not want to face this day.

Our U-Haul, surrounded by mud puddles, is sitting forlornly in front of the house as we drive up. A fire ant hill is directly in front of the house. It has been there for quite some time as it is about two feet tall.

"Hey," calls a voice from the house across from us, "stay away from those ants, their bite will raise welts." I turn to see who is calling. A thin woman in jeans and an old torn shirt, older than I am and no more than five feet tall, is walking toward me carrying a shovel.

"Ants can tolerate a good bit of rain. I'll stir them up," she says as she breaks up the hill. "I brung some instant grits," she continues as she sprinkles the white grits all over the anthill. Ants are scurrying around, carrying their eggs. "The grits swell in their stomachs and kill them.

"Ya had breakfast yet? Come over yonder, I got coffee on the stove and grits in the pot. By the way, my name is Lizzie." She holds out a calloused hand, which I take in mine.

"Elena and Kai, we got here last night, but it was pouring."

"Yep, it's the rainy season." She leads us into her house. Her house has the same floor plan as ours, but scrubbed clean, the floors waxed and a hand-plaited rug covers the living area. The sagging sofa next to it has a bright-colored Indian blanket thrown over it. I notice she has a phone on a table made out of an old electric spool and an old rusty metal lamp with a bare bulb that has no shade.

Old wood chairs, none of which match, surround a table made out of an old door set on a couple of sawhorses. Oilcloth covers the top with flowers, freshly picked from her garden, in the middle of it. There is a freezer in the corner. The top is missing, and old blankets cover it to keep in the cold.

Lizzie pours steaming coffee into some brown mugs and sets them in front of us. "Glad to git some new neighbors. The old ones were a couple of bachelors. I am sure the house is a mess. They both got fired for drinkin' on the job and left in a hurry. I'll be mighty glad to hep ya if I can, seein' y'all have that bum leg." She dishes out grits into two bowls. "Sorry, we don't have any butter fer it." We gobble down the grits, drink the coffee and are thankful for Lizzie's kindness.

The sun is not the only thing brightening my day. Lizzie has brought my spirits back up.

"Why doncha sit right here while Kai and I see what needs to be done to your house," Lizzie says. I start to protest, but she insists. "Please let me be a good neighbor. I know how hard it is out here."

How hard is it, I wonder. What does she know that I do not? If I had only taken that warning to heart, I would have caught the first bus back to Atlanta!

The Reservation
Saturday
Kai

If I had known it would be this bad, I would have come out here first and gotten this place ready before I brought Elena. No one told us it would not be ready to move in. Elena never wanted to come in the first place. She did not need this nightmare. Lizzie is very willing to help. Lizzie seems like a good neighbor. I wonder who lives in that other house. There is a truck in front of it, and I saw someone look out the window, but no other sign of life.

The Reservation
Saturday
Hector (the recluse in the middle house)

Good thing I looked out this winda'. Folks are moving in next door. Those other rascals moved out in a hurry after the warden fired them. Just up and took off. Good riddance if you ask me.

That Lizzie is at it again. She is always messing with every new bunch that comes here. That big ape looks black to me with that pretty, white wife. What was she thinkin' marrying a big black ape like that?

Damn, she is a looker! She is a little thin for my taste, but that red hair and angel face, I could really go for a piece of that.

I wonder why she has that cast on her leg. That black ape probably broke it for her. Ya caint trust his kind. Uppity blacks always think they are better than white folk. Got his self a real trophy thar! He must not be from around here. Our black folk knows their place.

That ape needs to get his self back on his own side of the tracks and stop messing whar he don' belong.

I will catch that little red-haired filly some time, and show her a good time. Yep, I sure will! That black ape will have to go to work sometime. Then, I can have her all to myself.

Man, she sure got a load of belongin's. And there's that dern Lizzie helping herself to a bunch of it. Nobody ever gives me anything. I got all I needs anyhow. Jest so they leave me alone.

The Reservation
Saturday
Kai

The trees look like pecan trees. It looks as though we may get a good crop. Three of these trees are right by our house, three by Lizzie's house, but only one on the other side of the unknown neighbor. Behind the houses, there is a rather broad field of planted crop, beans maybe. Lizzie has a garden behind her house staked out with a string all around it. It may be too late to start a garden. Everything seems to be ripe already. The season here is much earlier. We will have to check with Lizzie to see what we can plant.

Now that we got the house hosed out and dried, I re-hang the kitchen cabinet doors. It looks a lot better. John Lizzie's husband has come off shift and, after introducing himself, is helping to arrange the furniture we bring in from the U-Haul. It is good to have someone to help me carry things.

Between Elena and me, we have more stuff than will fit in the house. John has claimed the old single beds from the house for his two boys. Lizzie is applying a coat of silver paint and the beds are drying out in the yard.

As we remove each new article from the U-Haul, Lizzie is hoping it will not fit in our house. By the time John and I are finished, about half of the things have disappeared into Lizzie's house, and a pile of her old makeshift items is stacked in the yard. John helps me repack all the leftover items from the pile into his truck, and we take them to a dumpster that we passed on the way in.

"Everything will be gone by tonight," John says knowingly. "Lots of folk need that stuff. That is where we got most of ours, raidin' the dumpster."

That is humbling. I am beginning to see how lucky we really have been. *Have been*, but what about tomorrow? Our money is mostly gone. Looking through my coat pockets, I find a few dollar bills, some quarters and other loose change. I remember the penny jar I brought along that is in my dresser. Elena says she has a coin jar too.

The benefits I need for Elena did not apply to her hospital bill. She had no insurance at the time. I signed her out and promised to pay monthly. That will need to come out of my paycheck each month.

We have Elena's credit card. I will use it to go to Forsyth, and I will leave what change I can for Elena.

North Carolina
Saturday
Mina

We traced Kai to Smyrna, which is a suburb of Atlanta, from the Department of Motor Vehicles. When Bob our investigator, checked, he had already moved. I cannot believe we can be just a step behind him. If he would just leave forwarding addresses, it would help. Of course, Kai does not know Mark and I are looking for him. People are supposed to change their address on their driver's licenses, but most just let them go until they need to be renewed. Kai's birthday is coming up, but I do not know what year he needs to renew it. Bob is optimistic about finding Kai now. It will be soon.

Mark is happy with his job here at the base. He has a great crew working with him. We have more money now that his rank upgraded. With the allowance for the children, we have all we need.

I am used to this life in the service. It suits me fine. Flight has friends now, and he has become an extraordinary helper for his age. I never knew a little boy could be such a companion. He seems much older than his years. Mark spends as much time as possible with the kids, which makes him such a wonderful father and gives the children an excellent male role model. Mark and I have never been happier.

The Reservation
Saturday
John

Kai seems to be a good sport, not like those jokers who lived in that house before. I can use a good friend out here. Lizzie and the boys can use some protection from that Hector that lives in the middle house. I will clue him in on Hector and the prison itself sometime while we are out fishing.

There is no need to bother the womenfolk with our rough talk. They are better off left to themselves.

The job here is not easy. They will put Kai as a rookie officer in one of the better dorms until he gets the hang of it, so I am not too worried. I will tell him about my job in the mental health section later. I do not want to discourage him.

Lizzie is so excited about all her new possessions. I can see now that I have not given her much. We love each other and the boys have what they need. A loving home is worth more to me than all the little things that money can buy. I know Lizzie feels the same way, but I wish I could be a better provider.

Chapter 12

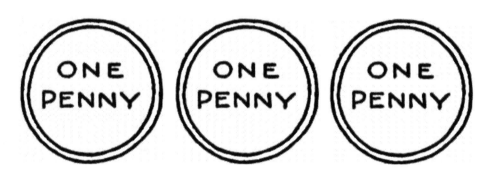

CROWDER PEAS

The Reservation
Sunday
Elena

The ever-present Lizzie, who now seems to be a fixture in our house, comes back with some coin rolls and says, "Let's count pennies. John and the boys are going fishin' down by the branch, so let me hep' you."

"Sure, why not?"

Kai comes out with a fishing pole and joins John as they load an old johnboat into the back of John's truck. John Jr. is fourteen and his brother Dan is twelve. They ride in the back with the boat as both men get in the truck and rattle off across an old muddy trail out to a pond.

So much for a honeymoon, I have Lizzie. Kai has John.

After the boys come back, we have a fish fry. They really caught a mess of fish. All of us are in a good mood now. We all eat our fill of fish and hush puppies that Lizzie has fried up and the men folk swap stories about the prison and Forsyth while Lizzie and I clean up and wash dishes. I feel more at home with good neighbors and friends like these. Maybe this move will work out for us.

Our last night together in our new house is bittersweet. We cling to each other as if there were no tomorrow. Kai has to get up at 3:00 AM to go to Forsyth. We both promise to spend as much time together as possible when his training is over. After Kai leaves, I sit with tears dripping into my coffee. I feel so alone and out of my element. Dawn is breaking and my heart with it. How did I become such a lost and dependent soul in such a short time? My aloneness has intensified by lack of transportation, a shortage of money, no phone and ten miles from town. There is no grocery store or anything here. I keep telling myself, *It is only for a short time, get over it. When Kai gets back, everything will be fine.*

Kai has the truck and our credit card, so he should have enough for transportation and lodging. I am glad I have that card paid off. It will be a lifesaver.

When John comes home, he drives us to town. I use my coin rolls to buy a ham bone and some oatmeal. John's gas tank is just about empty. I feel sorry I have nothing to help buy gas.

Lizzie has Crowder peas in her freezer that she shares with me and shows me how to cook them along with the ham bone. I am losing weight. With oatmeal for breakfast and Crowder peas for lunch and dinner along with some greens from Lizzie's garden, I am at least eating. Without Lizzie, I would be lost.

Once I scrub this house clean, there is not much else to occupy my time. I have no TV, but Kai's radio picks up a few AM stations that have mostly religious music and a lot of talk radio. All the news I ever wanted from an area I know nothing about: tobacco futures, the hog report, etc.

I reread every book I brought with me at least three times. Lizzie shows me how to cut up rags, and I start to braid them. I hope to have a rug like hers for my living room. It is not as easy as it looks, but just the industry of doing it makes the days go faster and helps fill out the lonely hours.

The cast on my leg has become an irritation. I do not have the transportation or the money to get to a doctor, so I decide to remove the cast from my leg myself. I borrow a hacksaw, a hammer and a chisel from John and cry a lot while doing it. It is more difficult than I imagined without cutting myself. Finally, I find my leg under all that plaster. It is pale and smaller than the other leg. The skin is as cracked as an alligator skin and peeling.

It was probably a bad idea to remove the cast, but what the heck. I rub cocoa butter on the offending ankle and step down gingerly on my foot. My leg and foot are full of pins and needles, but they hold me. I vow to use my crutches until the leg gets stronger. At least, all that extra weight is gone, and I can scratch carefully the itch that has been there for weeks.

Now that I am walking more, I am trying to explore a little bit of the area. I am afraid of the snakes that seem to be everywhere. The mosquitoes have become real pests but do not bother much during the day. Clouds of gnats, however, are something else. They seem to swarm around my face. As I try to shoo them away, Lizzie only laughs. Even though they get in her face, she does not seem to be bothered.

When a wasp stung me, Lizzie put toothpaste on it, which made it feel better. She seems to be full of so many country remedies I have never experienced. I have a large straw hat I wear to keep off the sun, but still I am sunburned. I wear sunscreen and stay in the shade as much as possible. Long cotton stockings cover my arms.

Lizzie and I catch some crickets and walk out to the pond to fish. Thank goodness, the fish likes the crickets. With the few crappies I caught and fried up, I feel that I have had a feast. Lizzie caught a whole string. (She says you have to hold your mouth just right and jiggle the pole to catch that many.) She happily cleans them and serves them to her boys with the ever-present greens.

Her children never seem to complain. Both boys are well behaved. I have never seen them argue. They are respectful of both Lizzie and John and polite to me as well. I hope I can raise boys like that someday.

Crowder peas seem to be the main dish down here. They are full of protein and take the place of meat. Greens come in the form of mustard greens, turnip greens and collards, all of which grow in Lizzie's garden. Lizzie thinks the mustard greens are the best. I have not made up my mind. We never had greens when I was a child, so I have not learned to like them even though I eat them here without complaint.

One day Lizzie made me a pineapple sandwich: white bread spread with mayo and a ring of pineapple. It was such a soggy dripping mess, but I ate it, glad to have food.

After living in Atlanta, the south Georgia cuisine is so different: more highly seasoned, more reliant on vegetables and much simpler. Corn bread is a staple. Not the sweetened corn bread with lots of butter we served out west, but plain corn bread made on the stovetop in a fry pan and cut into wedges.

I am hoping, when Kai returns, that I can find a job. I can drop him off for work and have the truck. Every day seems endless, but time is passing.

Kai should be home in a week and a half. My braiding of the rags into a rug is finally taking shape. It is nothing I can do commercially, but at least I have accomplished something.

The end of the month has arrived and, with it, Kai's first check. It is not very large and I cannot cash it without his signature, but at least there is beginning to be some hope for groceries. John brought me a squirrel he shot. After skinning it and boiling it into soup, I have a little more protein to last me for a few days. I pledge never to complain about any meal again.

My clothes have begun to hang on my meager frame. I could kill for an orange or some juice. Lizzie says she gets her vitamin C from the greens. Orange juice is too expensive, and she does not buy it often. Her children seem healthy without it.

Prisoners are beginning to work in the field across from the houses. They bring them on a bus that they park in the lane. A guard with a shotgun accompanies them.

Not knowing what to do, I stay in the house with the door locked. I peer out the window anxiously whenever I hear them.

Today, I hear the guard yell, "One more step toward those houses and I'll take out all three of you!" I cannot see what is going on, but I hear shouting and hear the bus reloading with the prisoners. As soon as I hear the bus leave, I rush over to Lizzie, my heart beating wildly. I see she has a gun on the table.

"I keep it here just in case, she says. No harm done, y'all need to keep a gun handy."

I search through Kai's belongings, but I do not find a gun. I know he has one, so he must have taken it with him. The first thing I will do when he comes back is to ask him to teach me how to use a gun. I will definitely feel safer with a gun!

Could I shoot someone? If I did, would I be able to explain it to the police? I doubt I could do either one.

The bus crews come from the maximum-security institution. They are the ones that have guards with them, and they are the ones I fear most.

The medium-security inmates from the smaller prison do the majority of the farming. These trustees work on tractors and in trucks without a guard present.

Lizzie says she has not had a problem while living here for the last eight years. No one she knows has had an incident with inmates other than the guards themselves.

"What you need is a big dog. That cat is no protection from anything."

"I am not really fond of dogs! What I need is a bigger cat! A tiger would be nice," I say facetiously.

"There is a big panther that walks through here at night sometimes. I have heard him yowling around some!"

Now I know I need a gun! I wish Lizzie had not told me about the panther.

Chapter 13

THE TRANSITION

Forsyth
First two weeks
Kai

Here at Forsyth, they keep us busy all day, but at night we return to the motel. Many of the trainees go out and party at night, but my funds are so meager I just go back to the room. Elena is always on my mind. I cannot wait to get back to her. A phone call is out of the question. We do not have a phone, and I cannot afford a long distance call. Television is my only outlet along with studying these *ten codes*. There is one for just about any situation.

The Marine Corps taught me how to shoot and take care of my guns, and I aced the firing range. Just a week and a half and I will be back to Elena. Coming here, we had to postpone our honeymoon, but I aim to make up for it when I get back.

Elena must be as lonesome as I am at night. She looked so devastated when I left. We need to start a family. That would give Elena something to do with her time. All she has is Kitty right now. Kitty is not much company.

The Reservation
Third week
Elena

What have I gotten myself into . . . not enough food, no job, no phone, no way to get around, and miles from nowhere and all alone? Feeling sorry for myself, I sob, "It's not worth it. No way! I'm going to find a way back to Atlanta or at least to civilization somewhere." Crying myself to sleep only makes my pillow wet and my eyes red.

I awake with a throbbing headache and swollen eyes. Someone is knocking furiously on my door. *What can they want at this hour? Jeez 5:00 AM.* Never trusting anyone, I peep out the window.

Lizzie, all perky and wide-awake, is causing this entire racket. Oh, no! It is probably a problem. I have had enough problems.

As I let her in, she gives me a quick once-over. "Wow! What happened to you?"

"Just feeling sorry for myself."

"Well, don't be. A job just came open for the two of us."

A job? Oh, how I have prayed for a job! Jobs mean money. I am all excited. "For both of us? Can we use John's truck? When can we start?"

Lizzie drawls, "Slow down, honey, let me tell you about the job. You may not want it, but I can carry you over. John is working second shift, so we can use his truck. The job is right here on the reservation. They are hiring some women to work in the dairy. Seems there is a grant to see if women can get more milk from the cows than having the inmates milk them as they have been doing. I already told Cyrus, the manager, we would take the job. Think you can do it?"

"We will be milking cows?" I gasp, not expecting anything like what I think I heard. "How many cows?"

"Only about two hundred or so, but there will be four of us. The dairy has milking machines, silly, so stop looking like a deer in headlights. We just wash the cows and hook up the milkers. The rest is automatic."

Well, that doesn't sound too difficult. My ranching days were with horses. How different can cows be? But two hundred of them? Wow! Sure beats doing nothing—might even be fun. "When do we start?"

"First thing in the morning, so get some sleep tonight. Get up at four AM, so we can be out of here by four forty-five. We don't want to be late."

Lizzie has a sack in her hand. "John just cashed his check, so I bought some coffee and rolls. Can I eat with you? John and the kids aren't up yet." She smiles as I start the coffee and get out a couple of mugs. "We will have a lot of fun together at the dairy."

I wolf down a roll while waiting for the coffee. "Mumph," I say with my mouth full, which makes Lizzie laugh. It seems as though Lizzie laughs a lot, seems as though I cry a lot. I used to be so cheerful and energetic and whatever.

My third foster mom always said, "Change your attitude, young lady, or I'll change it for you." Do we ever outlive our childhood? At sixty-five or seventy maybe?

Chapter 14

Jobs at Last

The Reservation
Thursday morning
Elena

The day goes by slowly. I cannot wait to get this job, any job. I go to bed and try to sleep. When I am this excited, it is difficult to go to sleep. I know I set the alarm, but I wake up every hour and look at the clock. Finally, when the alarm is about to ring, I am sound asleep.

The alarm practically jumps up and down on the bedside table, waking me up. "It's four AM." Jumping up, I hurriedly turn on the shower. I have to smell nice for those cows. No phone, so it cannot ring as I get out. Rubbing myself down with a towel, I am now completely awake.

Falling back into my old routine somewhat like my Atlanta days, I fluff my hair and brush my teeth. What did I do with that lipstick? I decide the cows won't care. I don the clothes I laid out the night before, just jeans and a T-shirt this time and some old rubber-soled shoes. The dairy floor will probably be wet.

I am ready in record time, so I put on some of the coffee and drink two cups while waiting for Lizzie.

Lizzie and I bounce down the lane in John's pickup at four-thirty. The dairy is closer than I thought, only a mile. We could hike down there if necessary. An inmate in his white shirt and white pants with the blue stripe is driving a tractor down the road. He waves, and Lizzie smiles and waves back. As we pull up to the dairy, inmates are everywhere. I give Lizzie a look and she just smiles.

"No one is going to hurt you. All these are trustees, and most of them are from the sissy squad anyway." Not knowing what a sissy squad is, I keep silent. No sense in showing my ignorance.

In the dairy office, we meet Cyrus. "Hi, ladies, ready to start? I've got your paperwork ready so you can sign it, then you can let the cows in." Two other women come in just as we are starting to write. We make our introductions.

Janice looks a little older than we are with long brown hair in a ponytail with just a touch of gray intermixed. Lois looks very young, almost a teenager with short blond hair in a pixie cut. Both are very slim, dressed in jeans and Ts. It will be good to have some friends, if only at work.

It is hard to describe the odor of the dairy: bleach disinfectant mixed with cow dung. Black flies bother not only the cows but us as well. There are milkers hooked to their separate bottles connected by overhead pipes. We stand in a pit somewhat below the ramp for the cows. Rubber waffle rugs cover the cement floor. All four corners have trashcans with paper towel holders mounted near the milkers.

I am standing next to Janice, who says she has worked in a dairy before, so I watch her. One of the inmates switches on the milk machine, and a hiss of the suction and the hum of the motors make it difficult to hear. Huge fans mounted at the end of the barn help keep us cool, but add to the racket.

Each of us is responsible for four milk stations, with eight stations on each side. There is a ramp for cows on either side of the pit. This gives us sixteen milk stations to hook up at one time. Outside, automatic washers are cleaning the cows as they walk through. We also have hose sprays running so we can make certain the udders are clean and then we wipe the udders dry with the paper towels. We throw the wet paper towel all the way to the end of the pit into the open trash container.

The lead cows are making a racket mooing. With the hiss of the milk machines, the cow noise echoes through the space. The worker on the end of each side opens the gate. Thankfully, the cows know more about this than we do. They have come through here twice a day, and they are anxious to be relieved of pressure created by their milk.

Most cows are docile and patiently allow the washing, drying and having the milkers attached as though it were an important part of their day. I am on the end, so it is my job to open the gate to let the cows out of the barn.

As I release each row of cows, they all act the same way. If one licks my hand on the way out, they all lick my hand. I immediately fall in love with some of them. Other cows are in such a hurry to leave that they slip on the wet cement and almost fall. A young bull comes through the line standing expectantly. Somehow, he has gotten in with the heifers. We all laugh, wondering what the bull thinks he is doing.

Young heifers, their first time here, are skittish and harder to handle, like teenagers at their first prom, wondering what to do. Several cows are just mean. Like people, I think, trying to kick you any chance they get. One of them kicks out and cracks one of the glass jars. We close the entire system every time we replace a jar. The milk mess stays in the dairy and does not get into the lines. I am getting more efficient as the last cow is milked, but still much slower than Janice is.

Time has passed quickly as we are green and slow at this task. Janice is the only one who worked effortlessly. I am certain we will become more adept when we become as used to the routine as the cows are.

Our morning is not over yet, however, as all the lines need to be backwashed, the paper towels that missed the trash containers picked up, and the whole place hosed out to be ready for the evening milking. I am wondering why all the inmates standing around, could not complete this. They must have had this job before we came. They seem to be satisfied with just watching us work.

The milk is from Holstein cows that give milk with a low-cream content. There are homogenizers in a room adjacent to the dairy, and several inmates are working in there. They put the homogenized milk into large containers to chill rapidly.

As we go out through the office, I ask Cyrus when we need to be back. "Oh, just a few minutes before four this afternoon. You did all right for the first time, but you need to speed it up a bit. Oh, and by the way, you came in midweek, so you will have a small check this time.

"You get paid every week on Tuesday, so make certain you punch in and out on the time clock. If you do not punch in, you do not get paid. I forgot to tell you this morning, so I punched you all in, so punch out now and go home, and thanks, ladies."

As we leave, we see small calves drinking from bottles held by some of the inmates. Older calves are getting their milk in a bucket. I feel all the inmates' eyes on us.

118

After we get into the truck, I decide to be brave and ask, "What's a sissy squad?"

Lizzie is laughing again. "Oh, they're like you know, homosexuals—girl boys. They each have their own old man who protects them."

Good answer for a dumb question. I guess sex in jail is to be expected, I just had not thought about it. In fact, I have thought about sex, but I am not getting any. When Kai gets back, we will just have to have our honeymoon.

I have not had breakfast or lunch, but I am too tired to eat. Setting the alarm for three, stripping off all my clothes, I am asleep as soon as I hit the pillow.

When I get up for the second shift, I absentmindedly eat a roll I had left over. I am so stiff and sore I can hardly walk. *Limp* may be a better word. Not used to physical labor yet, I guess. Lizzie seems not to notice. She has been more physically active than I have.

The afternoon is a repeat of the morning. The stiffness goes away as we work. Our time in the barn has improved as we become more efficient. Lizzie and I both tire from this session and vow to take a shower and go to bed. Lizzie's boys will have to fend for themselves tonight.

For the last few nights, I have been dreaming about food, for some reason, mostly about bananas. My dream this evening is about sex. Kai seems so real that I reach for him and wake up disappointed. I get up early and eat the last of my leftover rolls. They have become so hard they are almost petrified.

I do not usually get up this early, but I have a problem that all my jeans have become so loose I can hardly wear them. I am glad I brought this sewing machine with me.

I am not an excellent seamstress, but I have to do something about my clothes. I thread the needle and bobbin with strong blue thread and take in a pair of my jeans. The jean material is hard to sew, but I need a pair that fits.

Doing the best I can, I alter the size 6, cutting about three inches off the waist and seat, and re-sewing the French seams, double stitching everything. The alarm is ringing as I am finishing, so I put on the jeans and a new T and get ready for the cows.

Now, at least, I am too busy to be lonely, but this morning I was so stiff and sore I can hardly get out of bed. Muscles hurt that I did not even realize I had. My shower helps a little, but I can hardly get dressed, and reaching down to put on my shoes really is painful.

The morning is already hot, much hotter than Atlanta, with more humidity. I put on my thinnest T, but I know better than to wear anything but jeans.

After glancing in the mirror, I change my T because it looks too thin, and when I sweat, it may become transparent. There is no air-conditioning in that dairy, but at least there are those big fans.

The morning milking goes much better than the day before. After the first few cows, my muscles relax. One of the cows needs an antibiotic shot. She has mastitis and is too sore for the milker. One of the inmates shows me how to milk her by hand into a bucket.

The inmate is a big man, and he looks well fed. When he gives the shot, he looks at me first, I guess to see if I am watching, but I cringe, thinking he might be going to stick that big needle into me. It takes a lot of force to put that needle through the tough cowhide. The cow lets out a bellow but stands her ground. Poor thing is miserable, and I am sorry for her. I pat her on the way out, and she licks my hand. I make a mental note of her number, so I can see how she is doing the next time around. The cows all have numbers that are on a tag clipped into their ears.

We have begun to record the number and the amount of milk each cow gives on a chart. (Grants always need statistics. To justify our jobs, I suppose.)

An inmate tells me they are hiding one cow that fails to get pregnant. "What happens if she doesn't?" I ask.

"She gets taken to the slaughterhouse and made into beef," he replies.

Animal cruelty comes in all forms. Dairies breed cows as often as possible so they will give the most milk, their babies separated from them almost immediately, and the mother put through the torture of mechanical milking.

When they quit giving milk and cannot get pregnant, the prison slaughters them. Not much of a life! "How do you kill them at the slaughterhouse?" I ask.

"We take a sledgehammer and hit them in the head," he said.

I am sorry I asked. That does it for me. Cows are loving animals just like horses, not like chickens or fish. Not that I want any animal to suffer. It brings tears to my eyes, and I vow to stop eating beef or pork and to avoid buying leather items. I tell this to Lizzie on the way home, and she thinks I am being silly.

"Cattle and pigs are here for us to eat, and we have to wear shoes and belts," Lizzie says. I do not argue but I think otherwise and say nothing more.

At the afternoon milking, the poor cow with the mastitis is in my line again, so I hand-milk her. I am getting faster at this. I give her a treatment, and she seems to be getting a little better. I never thought I could care so much for cows. Milking is becoming automatic for me, which gives me plenty of time to daydream. My wet paper-towel throw to the trash baskets is becoming more accurate. I am pretending they are basketball hoops. I give myself two points for every throw that lands.

The flies are terrible this morning, and the hot cows and the heat are making everyone lose a lot of fluid. No rest breaks unlike what we had in the office. The cows just keep coming until the line ends. Today is Thursday—five more days until payday. Dairies must milk cows twice a day, every day including Sunday. At least on Sunday, the inmates will milk them, and we will have a needed day off. I know I will need the time to work on my neglected housework.

Cyrus has been talking about milking the cows three times a day. Maybe they will give more milk that way, but who is going to do all that milking? We are tired just with the two shifts. Everything is about production, maybe someone should ask the cows.

The Reservation
Peeking out his blinds that evening
Hector

I ain't seen that black man around here for a while, just that red-haired neighbor. She seems to be comin' and goin' with that Lizzie twice a day. She always has that dizzy Lizzie with her.

If she gets by herself sometime, I am gonna tell her a story, a big one. I'll ketch her outside alone. I just gotta stay cool until she do. She leaves her blinds open at night. I got a good look or two. I get hot just thinkin' bout it.

I'll ketch her, just wait and see. Lizzie goes to bed early, and John is gone until midnight, so Red and I can have a good time. Maybe tonight!

Chapter 15

HOME AT LAST

The Reservation
Friday afternoon
Elena

Friday, I come home and find Kai's truck in front of the house. The door is unlocked, and when I open it, Kai scolds, "Where have you been? I could not find you, so I went over to John and Lizzie's house, and they were not there either. I was afraid you had left me. I didn't know what to do, so I just waited here."

Tears are streaming down my face. This definitely is not how I imagined Kai's homecoming. I am tired, sweaty and grimy. The heat has plastered my hair to my head, and I smell like the barn.

Defensively, I snap back, "I took a job because I was starving. Your first check came, but I could not cash it. I had no word from you, so how could I know when you would be back. There is no food in the house, so I hope you brought some. My payday is next Tuesday, and that is just for part of a week.

"I have had a bad time, Kai, I am sorry if I yelled at you. You just surprised me, and I know I am a dirty mess. I have missed you so much. Please forgive me for being a shrew!"

I am crying a flood by now as Kai comes over to comfort me. "Sorry, hon, I was upset when I couldn't find you." He notices my dirty shirt and jeans. "Where are you working that you get this dirty?" I push him away and head for the shower. The hot water revives me as I wash my hair. As I am toweling off and looking for some clean clothes, Kai comes up behind me, holding my breasts as he nuzzles the nape of my wet neck. "No need for clothes, I like you just the way you are. I am so sorry you had such a hard time. I'll make it up to you, I promise."

All thought of food or even talk has vanished as I undress him hungrily, kissing each part of him as I uncover it. Kissing and squirming against him until I can wait no longer, I mount his throbbing desire. Our lovemaking is almost brutal as we roll together in bed, hearts pounding, locked together at last as one. Both of us are exhausted, me from work, and Kai from driving. Apart too long with no communication, we are at last together, husband and wife.

We are soon asleep, naked in each other's embrace.

Some time in the night, I awake and shiver. Setting the alarm for four, I get a blanket, throw it over Kai and climb back in beside him. He stirs and murmurs, "I love you," and goes back to sleep. I am awake now. My mind is racing. I know I will have to leave him in the morning. That will be so difficult. I just want to lay beside this man forever.

Snuggling his back while he sleeps, I settle down a little, but my desire for Kai keeps growing and I can sleep no longer. Reaching around, I began to caress his hairy chest, and the hard nipples excite me as I rub against him. Kai moans, rolls over and is wide-awake. "I didn't get enough, either," he murmurs as he takes me in his arms. "Now, it's my turn."

His kisses are demanding, and his hands are touching me, those gentle hands I love so much. Heaven is here in his arms. Sleep is no longer important or even thought about. Longing and loving are the only purpose of our being. Neither of us can get enough of each other as we make love the rest of the night.

The alarm rings, and I break away from him, leaving him with a kiss. "I've got to get ready for work. Lizzie picks me up. We work in the dairy. I will be back around eleven this morning. You can sleep until then if you want. I still have some coffee, so I will put a pot on. Your paycheck is on the dresser."

The Reservation
Saturday morning
Kai

Tired as I am, I cannot go back to sleep. Drinking the coffee revives me as I plan my day. Somehow, I have to put some food in this house. Elena has had such a miserable time. No wonder she was crying last night. She is so damn thin. I have to take better care of her or she will leave.

Milking cows! I never expected she would have anything to do with a job like that. The house is spotless. She must have spent hours scrubbing it. The floor shines like a mirror. This rug on the floor is new. I have not seen it before. It looks handmade. Lizzie must have taught Elena how. It is very much like Lizzie's.

I wish we had some curtains for the windows. Oh, we do have curtains over on the dresser. I guess what I need are curtain rods to hang them. The old truck has enough gas to get into town. Stores probably do not open until ten, so I guess I will just put my things away and wait for her to come back at eleven, and we can go shopping together.

Where is that check? Damn, there is not much there! Maybe, we got a few bucks left on that credit card. Might as well wash my dirty clothes. I don't find any soap. The hot water will get them clean enough for now. I add soap to our shopping list.

Washing clothes reminds me of Granny washing on that old scrub board, singing to herself in her native tongue. What a happy childhood we had. She was strict with me, no fooling around, but Granny was cheerfully going about her chores, never complaining that she had to care for a motherless boy who's Mama did not want him.

No baby mamas for me. Not ever! Marriage and a family is the only way. I will never leave Elena and my child. Never!

The clothes keep me busy, but the time just drags. I cannot get Elena out of my mind. That month without her just about killed me. She just cannot leave.

Finally, it is eleven, but no Elena. I am pacing up and down, nervous as hell. I have had too much coffee on an empty stomach, which is growling. *Damn, I need Elena now.* Twenty minutes go by, and while I am still pacing and growling, John's truck pulls in with Elena and Lizzie.

The Reservation
Saturday morning
Elena

What a hard time I have, staying awake this morning! I need to get more sleep. What a day! The barn was hot. The cows were hotter. Next time, I will wear long sleeves to keep those flies off my arms. They really know how to bite!

Kai picks me up and spins me around as I come through the door. He starts undressing me before I can say anything. "Hurry, honey, get your shower so we can go to town. I will try to leave you alone long enough. No, I'll put you in the shower myself." He throws my clothes in the washer on the way and kisses my naked breast as he does. As tired as I am, I want him, but he behaves himself and puts me gently in the shower. Hurrying, I rinse off the barn smell and find some clean jeans and a T.

We jump in the truck, and we are off. This is the first time he has been to this small town: grocery store, one stoplight before the main street, then the bank, and a lone palm tree behind the post office. A hardware store, IGA, and lawyers' office just about complete what is here. Kai has measured the windows and stops at the hardware store to get some curtain rods. He pays for them with our credit card. We turn back and stop at the first grocery store. The State check is good with ID, so we fill our cart with the basics. We remember the laundry soap and soap to wash the dishes. I insist upon orange juice. Kai wants beer, so we splurge and buy a six-pack.

Checking out, we have a few dollars left, so we put on some gas and rattle home in Kai's old truck.

We open the bread and eat some with nothing on it, happy to have something. It tastes as good as when I was a kid. We fool around like a couple of kids on the way back to the reservation. It is great to have Kai home at last.

The Reservation
Peering out his window, Saturday night
Hector

Damn. I should have caught girlie last night. That big black ape is home again. That puts a challenge into the game. I will wait until he goes to work, and then let the game begin.

Looking at her is just about as good as doin' her. I get hot either way. She curls up in bed in that short nightie, and I feel like opening the window and crawlin' in with her.

I gotta get some sleep now, anyhow. If I fall asleep at work, they will can me. Goodnight, Red, I will do you in my dreams.

Chapter 16

EIGHT GATES FROM ANYWHERE

At the Prison
Sunday afternoon
Kai

John was right. He told me that with all the gates to get to the dorms, I am eight gates from anywhere. The nearest the inmates get to the outside is eight gates.

It is my first shift here, and I want to make an impression. I asked for the morning shift so my hours and Elena's would coincide, but that may not happen for a while. Choice of shift goes by seniority. Afternoon shift and graveyard are the two least popular so that is what the rookies get. I guess I am stuck with afternoon. It is better than graveyard at least. With no air-conditioning, the afternoon when I get here is the hottest. Large fans at the end of the dorm merely circulate the hot air. Those little rubber fans they give the inmates do not do much. Tempers flare up in this heat.

A fight broke out when I first got here. I thought my size might make a difference, but I had to call the squad to break it up. The inmates do not know me, so they had to test me to see what I would do. They seem to know I am a rookie.

Now that they know, it backfired on them, and they gave themselves a lockdown. There will be no privileges for anyone tonight. Everyone is yelling for ice.

It is lights out in a few hours, so I see how much ice I can give out before that time. That gets me some respect from the cellblock. Even though they are tough thugs, they appreciate anyone trying to help them. It seems that the thing they want most is just attention. Like little kids, they all want recognition. If I were in here that is probably the main thing, I would want also, someone to pay attention to me.

Men in cages must be similar to animals in cages. Neither does well in captivity. I always feel sorry for the apes in the zoo. I will make a point to give these men as much of my attention as I can without spoiling them. The human animal demands some respect, and if these men show me some respect, I will reciprocate.

The bugs in here start to move around in the dark. I put rubber bands on my pant legs to keep the palm roaches from crawling up. It really creeps me out.

As soon as there is an opening, I am going to reapply for the highway patrol. I have not told Elena yet. Elena despises this place although she seems to like those cows.

She is always talking about number 600, whatever that is. Elena is afraid they will butcher that cow, as she has not birthed a calf in a while. Soon, number 600 will not be productive for the dairy, and the manager will send her to the slaughterhouse. Now that Elena works at the dairy, she refuses to eat meat anymore. Elena is so thin. She needs something. I have to find a way to fatten her up.

The hardest part of my job is staying awake. I understand that if I fall asleep, I *will be fired*. Unless I make good at this job, I will not get into the highway patrol. The fear of falling asleep keeps me moving around and stomping my feet. The cellblock is quiet now. I just have to stay awake until twelve. So many thoughts are racing through my head that it is a wonder that I can concentrate at all.

I was surprised to see the control room manned by a female guard. She is a petite blonde. It hardly seems possible they would let such a small woman work in the prison. She informed me that her name is Peggy, and she has worked here for over two years, sometimes in one of the eight towers that surround the prison.

There is a double fence with two gates around the prison. The first gate has thirty feet of white rock before the next gate. She says the first gate is ours. If an inmate approaches the second gate to the outside fence, they are in danger. The order is to shoot to kill an escaping felon. The tower guards have shotguns and automatic rifles. The guards have orders to count to three and then, if no compliance, they shoot.

There are fifty-two inmates in my dorm, in three tiers, with the control room in between. The doors to the individual cells open and close from the control room or all cells lock at once. Tonight, Peggy locked them all.

Time drags, but when the shift is over, I hurry out to the truck. Elena has waited up for me. Neither of us will get much sleep tonight. We will make good use of these hours together. It may cut into our sleep, but so be it.

Chapter 17

Baby Blues

The Reservation
Two weeks later
Elena

I have a secret. I have not had my period since I have been here. I tell this to Lizzie who calls the doctor in Minton and makes me an appointment for next Thursday. "I will carry you over when we get through milking, no need to tell Kai until we are sure. It may just be the movin' and all. Have you been able to keep down your breakfast?" she asks.

"No problem yet, just this nagging feeling that something is different."

Milking now has become a routine. No more aches and pains, my body is used to the physical labor. My only issue is the schedule. We milk cows twice a day on time every day. Kai's schedule conflicts with mine. I cannot stay up every night until he gets home, and I go to work at 4:00 AM. Sometimes we only see each other in passing. I am off on Sunday, and he works that day. With our combined checks, we at least have enough to eat. Kai has one meal at the prison, so groceries last longer. I am amazed at how much he can consume and still stay slim.

We have fish regularly from the pond and Lizzie's ever-present Crowder peas. She feels she owes me for the furniture she got when we moved down, so Lizzie is paying me off in peas.

John and Kai have the same shift, so they have time to go fishing together and have become fast friends. Sometimes I am jealous of that because, with their fishing, I have less time to be with Kai. I do not want to be a nag, so I say nothing. I just let the resentment fester. Lizzie is always there for me, more than I want, but it never makes up for the absence of my husband.

There are female guards at the prison, and I sometimes wonder what goes on between them and the male guards. Kai talks about one in particular. Peggy said this, and Peggy did that. I have not met her, but I am curious. When I ask Kai about her, he is vague. "Just one of the guards," he says, "Nothing in particular."

"What does she look like?" I ask.

"Oh, you know, small, blond, looks like most of the women down here."

"How many other women have you looked at?"

"Jeez, I don't know. All I'm saying is they all look alike—not pretty like you," he adds as an afterthought.

Friday night, Kai did not come home. He is still not home Saturday when I left for work, but I am not bothered by that as he sometimes gets home after I leave. I am thinking he must be doing a double shift. That sometimes happens when no one comes in to replace him. John has not come home either, so Lizzie and I have to hike the mile or so to the dairy. The weather is fine, so we don't mind. Something must be going on at the prison.

The prisoners at the dairy are all abuzz. "Lockdown at the prison: some guards are hostages."

"What building?" Lizzie asks, but no one seems to know. Milking seems to take forever today as both Lizzie and I are worried about our husbands. We catch a ride with Janice. As we round the corner to the complex, Kai and John's trucks are in front of our houses.

We give a collective sigh of relief when we see they have made it home. Kai is stretched out on the couch, still dressed in his uniform, must have had a bad night.

Kai smells of beer. He is not supposed to drink in uniform, but there he is, in his wrinkled uniform, his shoes still on. He opens his eyes as I shake him, "Where have you been, I was worried about you and that lockdown at the prison." That wakes him up.

"Must have been after our shift. We went to a party at one of the guards' houses. We just got home."

Now I know I am going to kill him. "You and John?" I ask.

"Yep," he mutters and goes back to sleep. The couch is a good place for him. He may be sleeping there for some time.

I shower and get some lunch ready, slamming things around to get rid of my anger. I do not have a clean uniform for Kai, but it is his day off, so he can just sleep it off!

Kitty is hungry, so I get her some food, and she purrs around my legs. At least someone appreciates me. Kai can get his own lunch and get his own uniform ready.

Lizzie is out in the yard, smoking and pulling weeds out of her garden. She is perfectly calm. Guess she is used to this. The boredom of this place is getting to me. A baby will keep me busy and take my mind off this place. I miss Atlanta and the excitement of the city.

The fast lane was my refuge from my early neglect—a childhood no child should have to endure. Foster children, for the most part, have lousy childhoods, shuffled from place to place, living with people paid to care for them.

It becomes easy to use our childhood as a crutch, an excuse for future bad behavior. We need to put it all behind us and move on.

My thought fast-forwards to Corporate Headquarters and some of the other places I worked. I ate out at least once a week. Occasionally I would go to a movie and sometimes to a show at the Fox Theatre.

There is no movie theater here. Lizzie says there is one in Hazlehurst. She went to one once, but a trip there used too much gas. Lizzie has the added burden of having to stretch her meager income to include two growing boys. The boys are spoiled. They have good clothes to attend school, and toys for birthdays and Christmas. Lizzie and John are the ones who have to make do.

It is probably my fault I have become so isolated. With the dairy job, I have had no time for friends, just work, eat and sleep. I need a secondhand car, any car to get around. If I could get to town occasionally, go to one of the neighboring towns, maybe, and shop. I used to shop all the time in Atlanta, but not once here except for groceries.

Technology has passed this sleepy southern town by. I have become rusty anyway. We are so isolated out here on the prison farm. Still no phone, but I have no one to call anyway. Maybe depression goes along with pregnancy, if I am pregnant. I will find out Thursday.

Chapter 18

THE BETRAYAL

The Reservation
Saturday morning
Kai

Elena has gone to work again. She did not leave me anything for lunch! She just does not seem to care about the house or me. John and I should have come home rather than gone to that party, but we deserve to get away sometimes. The guard job is so boring, mostly just standing around. This is worse than the tour in the marines. The marines has more structure and purpose. This is just like working in a warehouse, only the goods in this warehouse are prisoners.

Peggy has let me know last night that she was hot for me. Elena is never home. I would not have touched Peggy if it hadn't been for all that beer. Now I feel guilty as hell. Elena would kill me if she knew. John better not let it slip to Lizzie. She has such a big mouth and is always over here. I cannot get at Elena without falling over Lizzie.

All I ever wanted was just me and Elena and maybe a baby or two. This is not it. With much more of Elena avoiding me, we will not be together that long. Peggy let me know she is available anytime. In some ways, she is much more exciting than Elena is.

I wonder how many other men Peggy has come on to. What about Elena? She said only women work at the dairy, so I guess she is not cheating although with this Lizzie thing, she couldn't be gay, could she? *Wow, my mind is way off base here.* Guess I should get some lunch and cool off. When Elena comes home, maybe we can work things out.

The Reservation
Coming home from the dairy, Saturday noon
Elena

Well, Kai seems to be home. Let's see what he has to say for himself. I am still furious that I spent all that time worrying about him being in that lockdown when he was just out partying.

I guess he deserves to be with his friends sometimes. Maybe I am just jealous that I do not have any. I am too tired most of the time to party. It would be great if I just had more time with Kai.

It is hard to do this job and get the housework done too. I guess I could ask Kai to help. He put up those curtains, and sometimes he takes out the garbage, but that is the extent of his help. He could throw in a load of clothes sometimes or help with the dishes. I am sorry I did not fix him lunch. He must be hungry.

"Lizzie, what did John say about the party? Where was it?" I ask as I get out of John's truck.

"You better ask Kai yourself. I think you have a problem with him."

"What's that suppose to mean, a problem?" Now I am curious.

"Oh, I think I've said too much already. You know how men are around women. But I heard Peggy really came on to him." Lizzie is looking a little smug and perhaps feels guilty for spilling the beans. "I am sorry I told you that, Elena. John told me all about it, and it just came out. Sorry!"

"Not as sorry as Kai is going to be. So it is Peggy! I am sick of hearing her name. I don't even know her, but you can bet I will make damn sure I find out more about her!" I growl as I slam the door and stomp into my house.

Kai is waiting for me, but I am too upset to deal with him now. He gives me a peck on the cheek and asks, "How was work?" I mutter something about same as ever and head for the shower. Water streaming over my head, I try to calm myself so I can, at least, talk to Kai in a civilized manner. Honesty between us has always been easy up until now. If I bring Peggy up, he may just deny it or, worse, become more involved with her. Maybe I should share my secret with him. Maybe that will bring him around.

As I get dressed, I call out, "Kai, I need to talk to you." Coming from the bedroom, I find Kai sitting on the sofa with a guilty look on his face as if to say, "Oh no, she knows." Sitting beside him, I take his hand and say, "I have a confession to make. You may not like what I have to say. We always have been honest with each other, but I have been keeping a secret from you."

"A secret from me?" he echoes. "You know about Peggy!"

"Now that you have brought it up, yes, *I know*, but that's not my secret." I am trying to remain calm with much difficulty.

"Lizzie is taking me to the doctor in Minton on Thursday."

"Oh, no, honey, I'm sorry about Peggy. How are you feeling? Are you sick? You have been so pale lately. I am so sorry I neglected you. So sorry about everything! Please do not be sick, I need you, Elena. I will make it up to you, please. I know I promised you it would work out, and it hasn't, has it?"

Kai looks so upset. It would probably serve him right if I did not tell him. As furious as I am with him, I am trying to keep my cool. Pausing deliberately, I let him sit there miserable for several minutes before I continue. "You are right about it, not working out, but maybe it will.

"Kai, I think I am pregnant. I will not be certain until I see the doctor. I wanted to surprise you." Kai looks stunned. Maybe he does not want this child. I know we always talked about having children, but maybe he thinks it is too soon. Kai says nothing for a while. He just sits. Then he stands up, pulling me up with him. Holding me close, he starts to cry. I have never seen him cry before.

"Oh, Elena, I am so unworthy of being a father. I promise you, I will be the best father a child ever had."

Well, we will see, I think, still being hateful about Peggy. "No more Peggy, or I'm out of here. I will not say this *twice*. I will just *leave* and *take the baby with me.*"

We have reached a truce of sorts. It will take me awhile to get over this betrayal, but I still love Kai, and I am determined to make this marriage work if not for me, at least for the baby.

No, a divorce is not the answer. I will not bring up a child on my own, no matter how disappointed I am in my husband. I will just make this work somehow!

At Home
Friday after the party
Peggy

My job is so boring. Good thing I can look forward to Kai on my shift. He is so hot. Most of the men here are so dull. That party was the greatest. Kai is such a stud. I cannot wait to see him again. He is not wearing a ring, so I guess he is available. Even if he is married, I don't care! She must be a *nobody*. Kai never talks about her. He does not talk about much of anything, but he has a gleam in his eye every time he looks at me. I have never met anyone this good-looking, at least not here at the prison.

Kai seemed interested in my daughter, Susan. He would make a good father for her. She seems to miss her daddy. I guess all little kids need a daddy, especially little girls. My dad was never there for me either. He was drunk most of the time. That is probably why I got married in the first place. What a big mistake that was. I married a man that was even worse than my father was, if that is possible. My husband was abusive to me almost from day one. The divorce was the best thing I have ever done.

No more marriages for me, I will not make that mistake again. I might live with someone, someone like Kai, but I will never tie that knot again.

My ex was so mean to me, and Kai is so gentle. I just love his big hands. It was a big mistake to get that drunk and had unprotected sex. I will not be so stupid next time, and believe me, there will be a next time.

"Kai, you are going to be mine. I usually get what I want, and I want you. Kai, you stud!"

In the Prison
Monday
Kai

Peggy keeps asking me over to her house. It is difficult to avoid her as she works the control room of my dorm. I have told her about Elena. She just cannot understand that I love Elena. She does not care that I am married. Hell, she is so sexy and so available it is hard to say no, and I hold out most of the time. I was resisting her advances until Elena started pushing me away to punish me for cheating. She has said no every time I have approached her.

143

Sex with Peggy is so different, almost savage. *If Elena would just not keep pushing me away!* Peggy has worked out a schedule, so we can have sex before work. That way, she says, I will not come home smelling like another woman. I said no at first, but she kept pushing, so I finally gave in. Hell, it is exciting, but I am not sure the guilty feeling is worth it.

Peggy has this adorable little red-haired girl, Susan. I wish she were mine. Susan is so loving and kind and looks so much like Elena that she could have been hers.

My life seems so complicated. This is not the life I want. I will just have to give up Peggy. Next time, I will tell her to leave me alone.

At Home by Herself
Monday night
Susan

Mommy, how come you leave me alone? I am just a little girl yet. It is so hard to stay alone, especially at night. You used to have a babysitter for me. Now, you just say, "Be a big girl." I wish I had a Daddy like everybody else.

Mommy keeps bringing different men home, and I am supposed to stay out of the way. Mommy and these men drink a lot of beer and stuff.

144

They do not think I hear them, but I know there is something going on in Mommy's bedroom after they come over.

Mommy used to pay a lot more attention to me, but after Daddy left, she seems so different. I really do not know how to tell her. Daddy was always so mean. I do not miss him. I just wish I had a real daddy like my friend Sara has. Sara's daddy is always around. He plays with Sara, and she seems so happy. I am so sad.

Mommy, please find me a real daddy. That man, Kai, you had over here seemed real nice. He told me I was very pretty. I liked him. Maybe he could be my daddy. With a real daddy like the one Sara has, maybe, I would not be alone at night.

I will ask Mommy in the morning about Kai. She may not like it if I ask, but I will ask anyway. Yes, I will!

Going to Minton
Thursday morning
Elena

Thursday is here at last. Lizzie is as excited as I am about the prospect of a baby. She has those two boys. She would have liked a girl, but it did not happen. She cannot afford to have any more now. Besides, she thinks she is getting too old. I listen to her chattering away, thinking I would like a little girl too, just the way I have always dreamed about: a little girl with red hair like mine. Of course, that will not happen. Kai is so dark. I would settle for a nappy-haired little boy who is dark like his dad. If he is as good-looking as Kai, that would not be so bad either, maybe we could have one of each.

The office in Minton is old with peeling paint on the outside and scuffed tan walls on the inside. Its tiny waiting area is already full of patients. When I sign in, I ask how long before I can see the doctor. "Oh, just a few," drawls the receptionist. "Glad you could stop by. Fill out these three forms and bring them back. Just wait a sec. I'm a-fixing to make a copy of your insurance card."

I lean against a wall, trying to write. There is no place to sit yet. Two women leave, and Lizzie grabs both chairs. I turn in the paperwork and sit down.

After forty-five minutes, I again ask about my appointment. The receptionist repeats, "A few minutes." After another thirty minutes, the nurse calls my name, weighs me and has me remove my clothes. She hands me a skimpy blue paper gown. "Make sure it opens in front."

I do not catch the doctor's name right away. He has a foreign accent I think is Asian or Indian. Pelvic exams always embarrass me anyway, so I am a little apprehensive.

"Congratulations," he says, "I think you going to be mama. We run blood test to be sure, and we call you." I give them Lizzie's phone number.

"How soon will you know?"

"Oh, Monday for sure, is OK, we sure you be mama."

Getting dressed, I come out and make an appointment for a month. I also receive a script for some prenatal vitamins.

The appointment card confirms the doctor's name, Mao Ye. Lizzie is excited on the way home. "What did he say?"

"He said, 'Is O.K. we sure you be mama.'" We both laugh.

The Reservation
Thursday afternoon
Kai

The girls are giggling as they come in. It must be good news.

Elena looks so beautiful when she is smiling. I do not see that smile very often.

"Well, let me in on it, what did you find out?"

"The doctor said, 'We sure you be mama.'" Elena is laughing now. "I won't know for certain until Monday, but I think you can count on it. We are pregnant. Dr. Ye is a funny little man, but I like him. He has such a time with the English language. As long as he knows how to deliver babies. There were at least four pregnant women in the office that looked as though they were due anytime.

"I am not certain when the baby is due, but sometime this fall. Dr. Ye will be able to tell next visit."

The ever-present Lizzie makes privacy impossible, so I just grab Elena and hold her close. "You'll be a good mama. We don't have that much to spend on a child right now, but there's going to be a lot of love, you can count on it."

Lizzie is standing there, grinning as though she is going to be the mother. I know she is happy for Elena, but I could really use the time alone with Elena now. I give Lizzie a nod, and she takes the hint. "Catch y'all later."

Elena has stopped smiling now as tears fill her eyes. "I wish my daddy was still alive, he would be so proud and mom too." As I hold Elena, I am thinking about Mina, wherever she is, and about how my pa would just not care.

"Shh, hon, we have each other. No sense in thinking what could have been. It ain't gonna help. I wish Mina could celebrate with us if we just knew where she is. We will have a dozen kids and a bunch of grandchildren before you know it. We'll raise our own town!"

North Carolina
Thursday
Mina

My children are growing. Flight loves to help with his baby sister. I was so certain I was going to have a boy for Flight to play with. It is just as well because Flight loves his sister and feels it is his job to protect her. I wish I had had a big brother to protect me, or any brother or sister at all for that matter. I wonder if all only children sometimes have that same hollow feeling as I do.

Family has always been important to me. I loved my mother so much that I let her raise my children. My future was so uncertain at that time, no job, not even a high school diploma. I could have taken them with me, but I loved them so much and thought Mama could do a better job. Mama did the best job she could in that old shack she lived in. She took good care of me, and I did not appreciate her sacrifices.

Now I have lost them and lost Mama too. I feel so sad sometimes. It is good that I have these two lively youngsters. It takes away some of the hurt.

Mark has become so involved with his job here that he hardly has enough time to do it and take care of his family. I know he loves us. It is the first time he has not been there for us, but we know how important his job is for the air force and the defense of our country.

Sometimes it is hard to be a wife of a man in the service, especially one as dedicated as Mark. I have been lucky so far. No major war has taken him from me. I pray each day that we will have peace.

Mark says it is necessary to have a strong military to ensure the peace of this country. I find it difficult to agree with that. A country with a strong military sometimes feels that it has the right to use its power against anyone that disagrees with it. It is a two-edged sword.

Sadly, we have no more news of Kai or Tanika. I am getting discouraged. The job of finding them is harder than I thought it would be. This is a big country, and they could be anywhere.

Chapter 19

PECAN WARS

The Reservation
Monday morning
Elena

On Monday, Lizzie comes running with the news. "The test came out positive for pregnancy. They thought I was you, and just said, 'Congratulations.' You better get those vitamins and remember you are eating for two."

"Yes, Mother," I reply. Lizzie is always telling me what to do. I might as well be her child. Sometimes, I think I am.

The pecans are starting to drop. They are paper shells, so easy to crack and just becoming ripe enough to eat. Lizzie says there is a good crop this year.

We see more squirrels in the yard now. A different kind than I am familiar with called fox squirrels. They are much larger than regular squirrels. Fox squirrels have a distinctive black-and-white color. I am looking at a fox squirrel now. He is sitting so quietly that he thinks I cannot see him. I sit quietly, so he becomes bolder and moves.

He quickly pulls up a wild mushroom, and pops it in his mouth. Then he runs up a tree and again freezes when he spots me. He blends in with the tree so well that you cannot see him unless you know he is there.

Lizzie and I have begun picking up the pecans from under the trees. Our neighbor, whom I never see, has come out to claim his share.

"Where the hell you think you get off takin' my pecans?" This skinny little man shouts at us. "The pecans on my side of the trees belong to me. Y'all have more trees than I have. I have been watching you, and you're takin' more than your share!"

According to this man, half of the pecans from our tree closest to his house and half the pecans from the tree on Lizzie's side closest to his house are his. To emphasize the point, he takes a stick and draws a line under half of each tree. After glaring at us for a few minutes, he stomps back into his house.

"Lizzie, is he always like this?" I ask. I rarely see this man. This is the first time he actually spoke.

"Yep, the pecan wars are starting again. He wants to start a war over those trees if you dare step on his side. One time, he even brought a gun out and pointed it at me."

It seems he is a recluse, only coming out of his house to go to work or to fight over something. I am not about to get in a fight at this point. "Lizzie, if he comes out again, tell him he can have all the pecans under that one tree of mine, if he wants. The squirrels get most of them anyway."

"If he comes out again, I'll yank a knot in his tail," Lizzie says. "He don't scare me none!"

It is strange that in all the time I have been here, I have never seen that man, except to see him peeking though his blinds. Lizzie says he works the graveyard shift, and his name is Hector Hall. I make a mental note to avoid Hector as much as possible.

Hector Hall has been acting weirder than usual next door. When Lizzie and I came home yesterday from our second shift, he was out prowling around wearing just his boxer shorts. We pretended not to notice him, but he was staring right at us.

The Reservation
That evening
Lizzie

This evening, when I was outside, I saw Hector peering in Elena's bedroom window. When I approached him, he ran back into his house, then came back out and jumped into his truck. As soon as John and Kai come home, I am going to tell them. Maybe one of the men needs to talk to him, or else I am going to report him to the warden. I did not tell Elena. She has enough problems. Elena gets upset so easily, especially now she is pregnant. We will deal with Hector ourselves.

The Reservation
Peering out from under his blinds
Hector

Wow, that was close. Lizzie may not have seen me, but I sure as hell saw her. The thought of gettin' caught is more exciting than just takin'

151

a look-see. I got a good look at Elena. Now I know her name. "Elena, y'all need to leave that big ape and come on over to my house. I will let you have all these pecans. You can have the whole damn tree. You can have all the trees, just come on over, darlin'. I will show you a real good time."

The Reservation
The next day
Kai

I rarely talk to Lizzie by herself, but she seems worried about something and approaches me in the yard. "Kai, we got a problem with that Hector Hall!"

"Who the hell is Hector Hall? I never heard of him. What is our problem anyway?"

"You know the guy in the middle house. He was prowling around in the afternoon in just his boxer shorts, and I saw him trying to peek in Elena's window last night while you were gone."

That does it. I am ready to kill this man, and I do not even know him. "What is he, some damn Peeping Tom? He had better stay away from Elena. Thanks for telling me, Lizzie, I will take care of him."

I am not certain what I will do. If I knock on his door right now and he comes out, I will probably deck him. That will get me in trouble. It would probably be worth it, but it might upset Elena. John and I will figure out something.

I talk to John, and then I approach Elena. I need to be very careful in what I say.

"Elena, have you met Hector Hall?"

"Oh, you mean the man who lives in the middle house? Yes, I met him. I am trying to avoid him. He came out of his house and accused Lizzie and me of taking his pecans. He even drew a line under both of our trees to show us where we could not walk or pick up pecans. He was outside when we came home just in his boxer shorts. I am afraid of him."

"Just *avoid* him. Make certain you keep the blinds closed at night when I am not here and the door locked. If he bothers you in any way, please tell me when it happens. I have talked to John. John says he will take care of it with the warden. John has been here a long time. I am just a rookie, so it will be better if John does the talking. If necessary, I will confront Hector myself."

"Kai, I hope you will not have to do that. I do not want you to get in any trouble. He just seems like a strange man with such weird-looking eyes. He is probably harmless."

I do not want to scare Elena about the window-peeping thing, but I knew I needed to say something. Lizzie may just be making up the episode about the window. She may just not like the man or wants to see my reaction. I hope that is all there is to it. With that thought, I let it go for now.

Chapter 20

Pregnant

The Reservation
One month later
Elena

Kai and I have worked out some of our problems. If only I can have a baby boy for him to take fishing with him like John does with his sons.

There must be more to life than working in this prison, but Kai gets defensive when I bug him about it. He is still waiting to hear from the highway patrol. If he gets that job, we can leave this place. I wish I could feel at home here, but so far, I have not.

Lately, I have been suffering from morning sickness. Lizzie says to take crackers to bed and to eat them before I raise my head off the pillow. This seems to help. I am careful not to get the crumbs into the bed! Orange juice will come right back up even though I know I should drink it.

A month has gone by as quickly as if in a dream. Lizzie again carries me over to the doctor's office for my checkup.

In the waiting room, I run into a woman with blond hair in a correctional officer's uniform. As I am waiting, they call her name, Peggy James. Oh! Can that be *the* Peggy? She is short and blond, which fits the description that Lizzie gave me of Peggy. She has a little red-haired girl with her that I would guess to be five or six.

When Peggy goes into the back, I sit next to this darling child and ask, "What's your name, honey?" She looks frightened because I spoke to her. "I'm Susan, but I'm not supposed to talk to strangers!"

"Good idea," I said smiling. "You are such a pretty little girl."

"Thank you, ma'am."

It is my turn to go in, and both Peggy and the child have left the clinic when I come out. That was such a sweet child. I would like one like her!

I am getting bigger now and beginning to show. Kai has been attentive to me, but I am afraid my new figure may turn him off. Peggy seemed so pretty, and I am jealous.

At Home
The day after the visit to the doctor
Susan

That pretty lady at the doctor's office looks just like me. She has red hair, and she was so nice. I wonder who she is. Mommy says I cannot talk to strangers. I wonder why not. Mommy asked me about the pretty lady, but I told her I do not know who she is.

I was afraid to tell Mommy she talked to me. Sometimes I just have to keep a secret. My friend, Sara, says that sometimes, we can have secrets from our mommies. Sometimes I have secrets from Sara too. I never tell Sara that Mommy leaves me alone at night. I never tell Sara I am scared. She would think I am just a baby. I am not a baby, I just feel so alone. Sara has a daddy too, so maybe if I had one, I would not be so lonely.

The Reservation
Late summer
Kai

Now that Elena is my lover again, I have stopped seeing Peggy. I am beginning to wonder what I ever saw in her. She has been hitting on John and one of the other officers. John will not give her squat. He is as faithful to Lizzie as I should have been to Elena. I feel guilt because I know I have cheated, but I am repentant and will not let it happen ever again.

Elena and I are becoming closer and working out the schedule as much as we can. I still cannot get on day shift. Before I go into work, I have spent fishing with John's boys. It would be great if Elena and I had a boy, but Elena would really like a girl.

The house has suddenly become full of tree frogs. Tree frogs in the shower, dead ones dried in the rug, in the laundry room. Not only are there tree frogs but also chameleons inside and on the windowsills. Elena insists that we catch the frogs and put them back outside, which is an endless job because they just get back in. They make such a terrible racket; it is hard to sleep, along with the cicadas chirping and coyotes howling. It seems that we are living in the jungle. I have encountered possum at night and a lone panther that I have not told Elena about or she would worry.

We have both seen alligators sunning themselves along the riverbank. The local kids swim in that river. The ponds have alligators, water moccasins, and small fish. The woods are full of deer, which John says we can hunt during the season. If I am still here, I would like to hunt in those woods.

When John and I go fishing, I have seen many wild creatures around the ponds. Wild pig tracks are in the mud around one of the ponds where they come to drink. I wonder sometimes if the Native Americans were in this area and what tribes they were. Were the Seminoles this far north?

Walking through the woods makes me think of North Carolina. The woods around our cabin were very much like these including the springs that John calls "branches."

Thinking of North Carolina always brings up memories. Sometimes I wish I could forget my childhood. The memory of my pa taunting me formed much of my reaction to life. Here I am, a grown man, but I cannot shake off his angry words, "That baby mama don' want her chile!"

At the Prison
Late summer
Peggy

What the hell am I going to do! Kai got me pregnant. I know it's Kai. I have not been with anyone else since my last period. Well, he sure as hell is going to support this child. It is all I can do to support my six-year-old daughter Susan. Child support for her is so slow in coming. My ex has been in jail twice for nonpayment. As if putting him in jail makes him able to pay, just what are they thinking?

As a Catholic, abortion is out of the question. Actually, birth control is, but what's a girl supposed to do?

158

I guess if anyone should be the father, Kai is as good as any. He is so handsome, so our babe is going to be cute. I would love to have a little boy, a little Kai Jr.

I have convinced myself that I want this child. Susan will love having a baby in the house. It is not right to raise a child alone, but I am not interested in marriage again. Once was enough. That divorce cured me of marriage, and I found out Kai is married to that dumb redhead. I wonder if she is the woman that I saw in the doctor's office the other day. She is so skinny. I do not see what Kai sees in her. She has a figure like a boy. He never talks about her. Just stares at my figure. He is so clueless when it comes to women. If he would stick around with me, I could smarten him up!

Well, I guess I will just have to bounce this one off Kai and see what he says. He called in sick, so it will not be tonight. There is plenty of time anyway. Four more months is a long time.

I wonder what they will say at work. Well, that is going to be our secret for now, at least until it begins to show. So far, it looks as though I am gaining weight. I may tell John though. I know he can keep a secret. If that sexy John did not have that dizzy Lizzie, I could go for him. He might be interested except for Lizzie.

Lizzie seems to have him tied to her apron strings. John has those boys too. I guess I will let Lizzie keep John. There just aren't that many good men around. My only hope is Kai.

Chapter 21

TROUBLE AT THE DAIRY

The Reservation
One month later
Elena

    The job at the dairy has become almost automatic. The cows come and go. New ones freshen and some have stopped giving milk, so they artificially inseminate them to start the cycle all over again. Sick cows are treated, and if they do not recover, they butcher them. Local dairies buy the bull calves to enrich their herds. They arc too valuable to butcher. Resident bulls are few and only used as the last resort to inseminate a cow that has not become pregnant.

Antibiotic shots are difficult to give because of the tough hides. We are routinely giving these shots, but a vet is on call for our difficult problems and difficult deliveries.

The prison not only has dairy animals but regular livestock as well. Little white birds follow the livestock around. Lizzie calls these cowbirds.

I have seen deer grazing along with the cattle. Kai wants to hunt them in season. Hunting to me is cruel, and I told him I would rather he did not. Kai looks sad but tells me he will not kill a deer if I feel that strongly about it. He may go with John just to help him carry his deer out.

Woods surround the fields that are becoming lush with crops: peas, beans, cucumbers, squash and acres of watermelon. I have seen Lizzie sneak out in the field at night to grab a watermelon. Although I have been tempted, I consider this stealing. I do not want to get in trouble or to get Kai fired over a watermelon.

While Kai is gone at night, I have been making a few baby clothes and knitting a blanket, yellow because I do not want pink if we have a boy. Yellow is my favorite color. The knitting is going slowly because I keep dropping stitches and have to unravel, but I am getting the hang of it. The bright yellow stitches show up and are easier to work with than a dark color.

Bright colors seem so much more cheerful than grays or beige. The entire interior of our house is beige. Not really white and not really beige—sort of a dirty white. The only thing we did to the house was to put up the curtains. We are not interested in the house enough to do anything with it. We ignore both the house and the yard. There is not enough grass in the yard to grow now that the rainy season is over, mostly just sand.

My life here at the prison has just become all right. I am not enthusiastic about it, but with the baby coming, I know I will have plenty to do. Kai and a baby is all I need.

Kai seems more approachable than before and more in tune with my needs. He told me pregnancy is making me prettier. My tummy is not as flat as it was, but I can still get in stretch pants. I have begun wearing my shirt outside my jeans. Unless you look closely, I just look like a slightly fatter me. My face seems to be even thinner, if that is possible, but my breasts have swollen to almost twice their size. I never did have big boobs. I have started wearing makeup. I do not know if the cows care, but Kai has noticed the difference.

I am falling in love with Kai all over again, and we have become lovers again.

I am still working at the dairy, but I plan to quit soon. The doctor has recommended that I stay off my feet as much as possible as my ankles have begun to swell.

One of the cows has been acting up, number 427. She is a beautiful cow and gives a lot of milk. The problem is she wants to kick. She gets this mean gleam in her eyes, so we have to be careful when hooking her up to the milkers. So far, she has not been at my station, but she has broken at least two collection bottles. She seems to know when she can catch us off guard. The dairy has been exceedingly hot. The smell and the heat combined with my pregnancy have caused me to feel faint.

Each day at the dairy, I am more exhausted. Going to work is more of a chore than it used to be. Some mornings, I would just like to sleep in. Petty irritations with my coworkers and with the inmates add to the stress.

Kai seems to be excited about the baby although I am not sure if he wanted a family this soon. We just do not have enough time together to stay connected as a couple. I leave in the morning before he gets up, and he is still asleep when I come back.

Lately, I have been lazy and gone back to bed with him. Although he is dead to the world, I like the comfort of sleeping next to him. With all my pregnancy problems, I just do not feel very sexy. If Kai could just get on day shift, we could have our evenings and nights together.

The Reservation
Two weeks later
Lizzie

I am worried about Elena. She needs to get more rest. Each day is such a chore for her. Her pregnancy is starting to become a problem. When I ask her if we should stay home, she always says, "No, we need the money." She is afraid that Cyrus, the dairy manager will notice she is pregnant and will make her stay home. She makes certain to wear very loose shirts to the dairy.

At the Prison
Early fall
Kai

Work at the prison has become easier for me. I have developed a respect for many of the inmates that are trying their best to make their lives productive even though incarcerated. Many are attending school, as they were high school dropouts. Getting their GED has been a major milestone in their lives. I found out also that there are many Vietnam vets here. That war did nothing but ruin the lives of many young men. They came back unappreciated and as unsung heroes. Many could not adjust to life on their return.

The trustees get around the prison by using passes, much like students use to get to different areas. The floors of the prison are ordinary concrete. The inmates make them shine like marble with multiple coats of wax and polishing buffers.

There is an excellent law library. Some inmates become knowledgeable enough to appeal their cases. They have the opportunity to work with paralegals. I do not believe every inmate is guilty of the crime as charged although most are serving time for valid reasons.

Many inmates here have several life sentences. Others are so used to incarceration that they cannot live in the free world.

Some do not want to leave. There is nowhere to go when they get out. Repeat offenders sometimes just do so to get back in the system. A good number of prisoners were abused children from broken homes or worse. Excuses are rampant, some are legitimate, but most are just excuses. One inmate told me he was not a criminal. He just killed his best friend.

Housed in this prison are the worst offenders in the state. Life here is tough, and some gang activity prevails. Fights are commonplace. Inmates have ingenious ways of making weapons out of common articles. Dental floss mixed with glue and metal fillings work as a method to saw on the bars. Spoons can be fashioned into knives. Even sharpened pencils serve as weapons.

The inmates tolerate thieves, murderers and armed robbers, but a child molester has to live in protective custody. Sometimes even protective custody is not enough.

HIV presents a new problem. We have separated these men from the general population. No one quite knows how to handle that disease yet. Some officers have quit because they do not want to work in that dorm. I am more concerned with tuberculosis as it is more prevalent. The older population is not a problem, only the new arrivals.

At the Dairy
One month later
Elena

This morning is like so many Indian summer mornings—not only is the dairy hot, but the black flies are biting the cows as well, which makes the animals restless. Even as hot as it is, I have been wearing long sleeves to keep the fly bites to a minimum. We really need the money, but I feel that in a few more weeks, I am going to give up this job.

The dairy manager has hinted that if I know how to type and use a computer, he may have an opening in the main husbandry office. He just has to get permission to proceed and to get the funding arranged. It is an extension office as well, so I would not have to put in another application.

My pregnancy is beginning to show although Cyrus, the dairy manager is not yet aware of it, and they may not want to hire a pregnant woman, fearing my longevity. I still have three months before I deliver, but three months would be hardly worth getting the extension service to hire me. I would like to be a stay-at-home mom with our baby.

Trouble has arrived—number 427 is at my station. She has mastitis because she has been so hard to milk. She seems docile enough this morning, and she stands patiently while I wash her and hook her up to the milkers. (I dumped the milk from the collection bottle into a pail rather than let it get into the system with the good milk.) After milking her, I have to put tubes in her teats with medication.

One of the inmates brings me the meds. I am so intent in placing the tubes that I do not see her foot until it has hit me squarely in the stomach. I fall to the floor of the barn. The pain is intense. The cow becomes so enraged that it takes two inmates to subdue her and lead her out, kicking all the way. I feel lucky she did not hit me in the face.

Doubled over with pain, I cry out. The dairy manager comes out from the office and runs over to see what the commotion is, but as he does, the barn seems to tilt. The world has gone gray. I am falling through space and then nothing.

Chapter 22

Weeping willow

THE WILLOW TREE WEEPS

Minton Hospital
That same day
Kai

A replacement officer came in to relieve me. The prison ambulance took Elena to the hospital in Minton. Not knowing all the details, I broke all the speed limits in going to Minton. By the time I got here, Elena had already been in emergency surgery to remove her ruptured spleen. The details are slow in coming as I sit and worry.

The hours tick away and still no report on Elena's condition. I have counted all the holes in the ceiling tile of the waiting room at least twice. All the magazines here are at least two years old, most of them *Newsweek*.

Surely, Elena must be doing all right, or they would have told me. After half a day of worrying, the surgeon comes to give me the news. "Elena," he says, "has survived, the baby has not. She just lost too much blood and went into shock. I had the baby on a monitor, and when it was in distress, we did an emergency C-section. It was a little boy, but it was just too small to survive, especially since its blood supply was inadequate. I am so sorry. We tried our best."

Elena is unconscious. I am almost in shock from worrying. We could have lost Elena. I do not know what I would have done if she had not made it through the surgery. I do not know how I am going to tell Elena she has lost our baby.

Guilt is hanging around my neck like a noose. It is my fault—if I had left this place and found a better job to support her, she could have stayed home. If she had stayed home instead of working at the dairy, they would have both been fine. My fault, I broke my promise to take care of her and the baby. My fault!

I call my supervisor, and he says, "Take off what time you need. We are shorthanded, but stay with your wife, at least until she gets home. Moreover, keep her out of the dairy. In my opinion, they never should have permitted a pregnant woman to work there. The inmates can take care of the cows."

Elena has been unconscious for hours. The doctor said they would keep her comatose for at least another day or until she gets stronger. Poor Elena, she has so much bad luck. This is such a small hospital. No private rooms, just doubles, but it seems clean, and the staff is efficient. I wonder how long they will keep her. There is nothing to do here. I might as well go home and feed the cat.

Lizzie runs over as soon as I get home. Now, I will have to answer all her questions. She starts in with the big one. "What about the baby?" I cannot seem to get the words out, but she can tell by the look on my face what has happened, and she puts her arms around me.

I have been able to hold it together, but now big wrenching sobs are racking my body, and still I can say nothing. I remember Granny telling me men do cry, as the willow tree weeps.

"Is Elena going to be OK?" Lizzie asks, crying now herself.

Getting my voice back, I tell her what happened and that Elena is still unconscious. "We won't know for a while how soon we can talk to her. I will let you know as soon as she wakes up."

"Don't worry none," Lizzie says. "I will quit the dairy, and take care of Elena when she comes home. I will let you rest a bit, but if you need me, just call. I'll take care of Kitty while you're gone."

"Thanks, Lizzie everyone should have a friend like you. Elena loves you like a sister," I add, happy to have Lizzie leave, so I can pull myself together. Going through the motions, I feed Kitty, and go lie on the bed, but sleep will not come as I worry about Elena.

I grieve for the baby. *Are we never to find happiness?* What have I done to have so much bad luck?

The night drags on forever it seems. Just as I doze off it is morning. Groggily I get up and shower trying to clear my head. Still worried about how I am going to explain to Elena that she lost the baby, I drive back to Minton.

A floral shop is on the corner, so I run in and get yellow roses. I know Elena likes yellow.

Elena is awake when I get to her room. The nurse motions me out into the hallway to tell me that Elena is not responding. "She hasn't said anything yet."

Back in the room, I reach for Elena's hand, but she pulls it back as though she is afraid of me. "Elena, it's all right, honey, I'm Kai."

Nothing I do pleases her. When I show her the roses, she looks a little more interested, but still says nothing. As long as she is this way, I am not going to explain about the baby. I will wait until she asks.

The doctor comes in and examines her, talking to her cheerfully and asking how she feels. He is greeted only with silence. "Well, you are better than you were yesterday," he explains. "You had us all worried."

Joining him in the hallway, I question him about Elena, "What is wrong with her? Is she in shock? Is she even aware she lost the baby?"

"No, the blood loss affected her brain and we have some damage there. How much, we are not certain.

"It may be some time before we know the full extent of her brain damage. We have not told her about the baby, maybe in time. We just need to take each day as it comes."

Brain damage, that scares me. I may never have my Elena back—first the baby, now Elena. It is as if they both died. This must be a nightmare. I will wake up soon and find it was all a dream.

Lizzie comes to the hospital, but she cannot visit with Elena as there is a *Family Only* sign posted. We meet in the hallway, and I give her the facts, as I know them.

"Yes, Elena will live, but she is brain damaged and unable to talk."

"God is striking you because of your cheating," Lizzie scolded. "How could you, and with that slut Peggy!"

That is the truth. It is my fault. Our marriage is ruined, my wife is brain damaged, and the baby is lost because of me! This is my punishment. Not fair, I am the one who should be lying there. Elena is innocent!

Chapter 23

HOME FROM THE HOSPITAL

The Reservation
Two weeks later
Kai

Lizzie is helping me bring Elena home. She still has not spoken a word. Elena smiles when she sees the house, and goes to sit in her favorite chair. "She remembers the chair, but not me," I whisper to Lizzie.

"Give her time, she will be all right, she has had quite a shock."

I have hidden all the baby things that we were putting together and warned Lizzie and John not to mention anything about the baby.

Lizzie makes some coffee, and gives Elena a cup. "Coffee," says Lizzie, "Elena, say coffee."

Elena looks at the coffee then at Lizzie and says, "Coffee."

"Good girl, Elena . . . this is Kai." Lizzie points at me. Elena shakes her head no. Shaken up by that rebuff, I go outside to talk to John.

"Lizzie is not working at the dairy," he tells me. "She wants to spend her time at home with her boys. She also said she will help with Elena, so recon you can go back to work."

"Yeh, I guess we need the money and Elena doesn't want me around. She seems to get along with Lizzie. Maybe someday she'll come back to me."

It has been days since I have put on my uniform. It seems too large. I must have lost some weight. Lizzie has taken Elena to her house, so I am alone with my thoughts.

Elena and I were so happy, and it all came crashing down on our heads. What else can happen? Bad luck seems to cling to me like a shadow.

At roll call, Peggy sits next to me with her come-hither smile and sexy body. The room seems to heat up as we sit there. I cannot believe she still has this effect on me. Elena is my only love. *Peggy just needs to leave me alone.*

"Can you come over after work?" Peggy looks at me expectantly.

"What's up?" I whisper. Peggy just winks.

Work is the same as ever: a shoving match that I have to break up, ice to deliver to the hot inmates with their never-ending petty arguments and with their pathetic little fans, trying to cool them down, cell doors slamming, the count, all accounted for, then lights out when all the bugs start crawling. Same ole, same ole!

Peggy is waiting for me at the gate. I have to get back to Elena. But Peggy wants to see me, so I take a few minutes, more than a few actually, and drive to her house. Peggy hugs me as soon as we get in the door. "I've got a surprise for you, hope you like it."

"What surprise? I don't have time today," I say, thinking she means sex.

"No, honey, not now," she says, reading my mind. "It's just like, well, it's that we are having a *baby*!"

"We as in *us*? No, I will not have it. I have Elena. There is *no us*!"

"There is now!" Peggy is upset that I am not happy. "You should have thought about *no us* before you got me pregnant. I am having the baby, and you will support us, like it or not!"

I slam the door on the way out. Damn it to hell, I have turned into my pa with a baby momma. Something I said I would never do, and what about Elena? What have I done?

What was it Granny said about willow trees, "They blow in the wind. They bend, but do not break. Be like the willow. Kai, my little willow tree."

I have not seen a willow tree anywhere. I need to talk to Grandpa Willow Tree as Grandma did. I sure need his advice. My life has taken a turn for the worse just when I thought I had already reached rock bottom. What else can happen?

The Reservation
One week later
Elena

Just because I cannot speak fluently does not mean I do not understand. I do know I lost our baby. Why will no one talk to me about it? They hid all the baby clothes I got from Lizzie, and the blanket I knitted and the layette I made.

I am so mad at Kai. I cannot bear to have him touch me. He doesn't seem to care that we lost the baby. It must be such a relief to him. He did not even say he was sorry about the baby, as though it did not exist.

Lizzie does not mention the baby. I know she cares. She just does not want to upset me.

Now that I have nothing to do all day, I am trying to braid another rug. My fingers do not want to cooperate. They seem to have a mind of their own. I cannot seem to read a book and remember what paragraph I started. Lizzie has a TV now, so when I go over to her house, I watch it. Lizzie thinks it will help me with my speech.

Most of the daytime programs are not worth watching. I like to listen to the news and the country music channel. If I cannot talk, maybe I can just sing my words.

Lizzie is upset today for some reason. She is such a cheerful person. It must be something John or the boys did. As she sits down beside me, she holds my hand. "You can understand what I am saying?"

I nod yes.

"John told me this morning that Peggy is pregnant. You remember Peggy, don't you?"

I nod again, more furiously this time.

"John thinks Kai is the father."

I drop the rug I am braiding and go to the bedroom and slam the door. So, that is why Kai will not talk about our baby. He has one in someone else's oven. Well, he can just go and chase his tail.

He is not getting near me that's for sure. Damn him anyway. All those things he promised, none of them came true. I am stuck here in my condition. I will just have to make the best of things until I get better. If that ever happens, I will leave him.

The Reservation
That night
Hector

Elena is leavin' her blinds open again. Wow, what a view! I wonder if she locked her door. Damn, she locked the door, so all I can do is jest take a look-see. "Just turn my way a little bit darlin', that's right, baby, and turn just a little bit more."

The window is unlocked. I can see that from here. It is a little high. I know I got a stepladder in my storage shed. Here it is. Now, if I can carry it over to that window without Lizzie or someone coming by—Lizzie's house is dark, so I think I'm safe.

OK, now I am in position. The window is stuck shut. My pocketknife will work as a wedge. "Here I come, Elena!"

Chapter 24

CONFRONTATION

Coming Home from Work
That night
Kai

There is someone outside my house. It is late. I just got home from work. I can see the outline of a person just outside our window. John may have forgotten something in my truck.

Opening the door, I find Hector Hall outside, peering into our bedroom. Elena must have forgotten to draw the blinds. In her condition, she may not remember what I told her. When I go back outside, Hector has his pocketknife out, prying away at the window and does not hear me approach as I pick him up by the back of the neck and shout, "What the hell do you think you are doing!"

Hector is a small man, and I have lifted him almost a foot off the ground. "I don't want no trouble," he stammers as he drops the knife to the ground.

"Well, buddy, you just found it." Blind with rage, I am ready to kill this little twerp. Just as I take a swing at his head, John comes out of his house, followed by Lizzie.

"What's going on, Kai?" John asks, the flashlight in his hand aimed at the piece of garbage I have in my hand that is whimpering like a baby.

"I think you better take over here, John, before I kill this scumbag."

Lizzie runs back in the house and comes back saying, "I called security, and they are on their way."

I need to get away from this place: away from Peggy, away from Hector Hall, away even from Elena. My life has become impossible: a wife who hates me, a neighbor that peeps in our windows, and Peggy who stalks me. Peggy is blaming me for her pregnancy, but I am not sure I am the father. She flirts with everyone, and with her loose morals, the baby could be the result of any one of her many flings. Peggy will have to *prove* I am the father.

The problem is what to do about Elena. We will have to move from the prison reservation if I take the highway patrol job. Elena cannot carry on a conversation, but she can take care of herself and do housework. She may be able to talk, just not to me. I know she is upset with me, but I cannot figure out why.

My last letter from my sister Tanika said she needs someone to help with her newborn twins. Maybe Elena could help. The twins would cheer

Elena up or at least distract her. She will be away from me. *I hope she will miss me!* I still love her but she is making it so difficult.

When I called Tanika, she said, "Sure, have her come up and stay with us, you know you're family, and if Elena can help me with the twins, it will be perfect." So I have a solution, for now anyway. I will just have to tolerate Elena until she comes around, or I get tired of waiting, whichever comes first.

Lizzie is at our house when I come home. She has been like a sister to Elena, but she is always under foot.

Elena can take care of herself now. I have to admit, I am jealous of Lizzie. Elena responds to Lizzie, but Elena will not even come near me.

"Lizzie, would you mind leaving us alone? I need to talk to Elena." That went over well. Lizzie huffs out the door, but at least I have Elena to myself.

"Elena, I know you can understand what I am saying, so please listen. We have to move from here. I will not be working at the prison after next week. We will be going back to Atlanta. We can stay with Jerome and Tanika until we can find a place." Elena looks puzzled, but says nothing.

"Please start packing your things. We will put our furniture in storage until we get a place of our own."

The Reservation
Moving day
Lizzie

"Elena, I wish you did not have to leave. Y'all have been such good neighbors. John and I have talked about getting a little shack in the country somewhere, but so far, it is just talk." I cannot tell her how much I will miss her, it would just make her cry.

"Do you want the furniture back you gave me?, I ask, "You might need it when you find a place."

"No, Lizzie." Elena is shaking her head back and forth.

"Thank you for giving it to us," I say with tears in my eyes. I know John will miss Kai. John had bought a deer license, and John and Kai were going hunting. Our boys love Kai almost as much as they do their father.

Elena is hugging me and crying, and so am I. Kai is waiting impatiently in the truck. Elena reluctantly gets in and waves.

Now that Hector Hall left, there are two houses empty. The warden fired Hector the night I called security. We will not miss him. I wonder what will happen next—something always does around here. You can count on it.

On the Road Again
Kai

The move to Atlanta goes smoother than I thought. The silence on the ride makes the trip seem longer, but I turn on the radio to keep me company. Elena is still not talking to me. I do not know whether she will not or cannot. I will not bother her, but when I get back from Forsyth, we will need to come to terms with our marriage.

I know where I am going, but the trip will still take as long. I am surprised that I feel I will miss this place. The tobacco fields are empty now, the red earth plowed in furrows ready for a winter crop, perhaps of cabbages or onions. Smoke is rising from the drying sheds, filling the air with plumes that become one with the cloud-filled sky. The trees are bare, and they are lifting their naked arms in surrender to the winter. Dry leaves are blowing across the road. The temperature is chilly although snow rarely falls in this part of the South. I had become accustomed to my work, and I will miss John, but circumstances and I believe the fates are taking us in a new direction. Where they will lead I do not know.

Tanika is on her best behavior when we arrive, and Jerome is at least civil to me. I will be going back for more training for the highway patrol again at Forsyth. That will leave Elena with the twins while Tanika goes back to work. Maybe the change will help Elena. The separation from Elena may be a good thing for both of us. We will have time to sort out our feelings and decide the course of our marriage or our divorce. That is up to Elena as I still would like to try to make our marriage work.

If nothing else, the escape from the prison is good for me. No more Hector Hall and no more Peggy. I probably have not heard the last from Peggy, but I can postpone the confrontation for a time.

Chapter 25

Back in Atlanta

Marietta
November 1984
Elena

Here we are in Atlanta, but under what circumstances? Atlanta is no longer my dream. Tanika has been cool but polite to me. The twins are cute but fussy. I wonder if my child would have resembled these two boys. Probably not, as I think they look a lot like Jerome. Kai and Tanika have straight black hair. The twins have fuzzy heads.

I am appreciative of Tanika and Jerome, giving us a place to stay even if they are doing it only for Kai. In my condition, I cannot go out to work, but I will do my best to take care of these darling little beings. Kai is not here, which is just as well. At least, Peggy is out of the picture for now. It hurts me so that Kai was unfaithful.

What did I do to deserve his betrayal? As I look back on my days in south Georgia, I should have stayed home and been the wife Kai needed. I was not there for him. I wanted him to adapt to my schedule. I could have adapted to his.

The few dollars I made at the dairy were not worth it. It cost me our baby. I will forever mourn for the child that could have been except for my greed for money.

What about Peggy's baby? If she can prove Kai is the father, she can saddle us with child support for the next eighteen years. If it is Kai's, will he get visitation and will he want to be part of Peggy's life?

I would like to try again for another child, but at the present, Kai and I are not even sleeping together. Maybe when he gets back, we can forgive each other. It will be difficult.

The twins are identical. They are still wearing their hospital bracelets. One says Jerry, the other Jerome. Jerome is a little bigger than Jerry, but that will probably change. They both are such long babies for twins.

Tanika has gone to work, so I am totally in charge. I am glad she trusts me enough to take care of her precious children.

In some of the foster homes, there were babies. I helped with some of them, so I am not totally without mothering talent. I am beginning to get some of my verbal skills back. While the babies are sleeping, I am practicing my typing skills using Tanika's typewriter. It is not easy. Once it was my forte, now my fingers are so clumsy. I make so many mistakes, but maybe it will come back in time.

Time is all I have for now, lots and lots of time.

I am writing a letter to Kai on this typewriter, asking for his forgiveness for not being a better wife, and for losing our baby. I realize now that it was my entire fault.

Even his affair with Peggy was, in part, my fault. A husband usually does not stray if he has enough love at home. He was not getting it from me. I was too busy making a few bucks.

When I became pregnant, I should have quit that job. I just did not realize it was dangerous. Maybe if I had been more careful, even that job would have worked out.

I do not know if we can get back to where we started, but maybe we can make a new beginning if it is not too late. *Please, Lord, help me get my husband and my life back.*

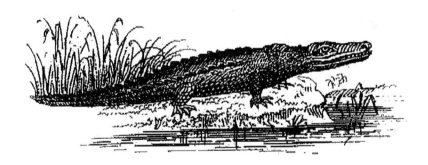

The Prison
November
Peggy

Kai left me with no forwarding address, but when he starts his new job, I can probably find out from the State. Our baby will be here in one month. It is getting harder to go to work now that I am getting bigger. My ankles have been swelling, and my blood pressure is sky high. Dr. Ye is worried about me. He says I need to quit my job and stay home.

I have obtained a desk job in the medical clinic until I deliver, which is much more comfortable, so maybe that will help my legs. These inmates are something else, always cutting their selves so they can come to the clinic to see the nurses. How pathetic!

One of the nurses got a little upset today when an inmate got too close and put his hands on her. She was not hurt, just embarrassed. They put the inmate in lockdown. It serves him right, the little creep!

Working at this prison for the last two years, I really have not had much social life. Everything I do revolves around the prison. The only time I go into town is for food. For clothes, I have to go to one of the neighboring towns.

There are so many funny names of towns in south Georgia: Santa Claus just outside of Lyons and Watermelon down by Manassas. My favorite is Watermelon Baptist Church. Pumpkin Vine is the name of a creek. In Vidalia, when the onions are ready, the streets just reek of onions. Onions are for sale all up and down the street. Onion eating contests, *yuck*!

Then there is Claxton with that rattlesnake roundup. They milk the rattlesnakes for their venom, then they have rattlesnake BBQ. The snakes around here are mostly cottonmouth, with a few rattlesnakes, coral snakes and kingsnakes.

A rattlesnake bit one of my neighbors. After he got over that he was bitten by a coral snake. He was lucky to live through that.

Of course, the worst part is the gnats. They swarm all over me every time I go outside. Alligators are in the rivers and the pond at the prison. My baby deserves better.

If I had any folk back in Kentucky, I would go back there. I liked the climate better, but it has so many bad memories. When I was first married, Ken always had to have his way. Then Ken started drinking. He became a mean drunk after Susan was born. He did not want to become a father. I knew then that we could not stay married.

I will go find Kai and find a place close to him even if he is still with that mousy wife. John says she cannot even talk anymore, and that she hates Kai. I will be Kai's woman.

I need to get some baby clothes. John says Lizzie had some she was fixing to give to Elena, but when she got hurt, the clothes came back to her. I am not proud. I will take them. I did not save any of my daughter's things. Another baby was the last thing on my mind at the time. Lizzie says not to worry none, she will babysit for me. I am not sure I am going to stay here. I may just try to find another job. Lizzie said Elena was fighting with Kai when he left, so maybe I still have a chance with him.

I cannot stop thinking about his gorgeous body and his quiet gentle manners. He is so unlike most of the men I have met. Why should Elena have him? I know I would make him a better companion. I am a better match for him sexually than that little mouse. Kai could not keep his hands off me when he was here. I could make him love me in time. I just know it.

He would make a good father for Susan. She seems so lost without a father. Susan has pointed out to me that all her friends have fathers. That would be the perfect ending for all this. Then we could all be a family, me and Kai and Susan and little Kai Jr.

Chapter 26

RECONCILIATION

Forsyth
November
Kai

I will be so glad when this training ends, so Elena and I can start over in a new place. At least, I hope she will have me. Lord knows how I will make it up to her. If I can be stationed somewhere near Atlanta, Tanika can help. If it is somewhere else, we will just have to make the best of it.

Most of this training is a repeat of the correctional officer program, so I can ace it. Some is new, however, and takes all my concentration. My training officers think I am doing OK although they have not praised me for anything outstanding. I am no hero, just a regular guy.

The following week

I found out today that my first assignment is to be in Cartersville, Georgia, which is only twenty-five minutes from Jerome and Tanika's house. Maybe my luck is changing. I could have been stationed anywhere. Cartersville is a small city, but it is growing rapidly.

Cartersville should have cheaper housing than Atlanta, and it is a beautiful area in the foothills of northwest Georgia. It is a big enough town for Elena and small enough for me. It should be the perfect place to start over if Elena will have me. *Elena, please forgive me.*

Tanika and Jerome are looking for a place for us. I would like something just a little out of town, maybe even a few acres.

North Carolina
November
Mina

At last, I think we have found Kai in Georgia. He is working for the prison. Mark called down there but just got the runaround. "Yes, he was here but he is going to another area. We will let you know if you leave your number. Are you family—His mother? Can you verify that?

"We need to get permission from the warden to give you that information. He will be out of town until Monday."

192

Talking to secretaries is not very productive. They do not have the authority to do much, or at least they pretend they don't. Certainly, we can wait until Monday for the warden. I have been waiting all my adult life.

If the warden gives us Kai's last known address, we should be able to trace him from there. Kai must know where Tanika lives. I need to find them both.

I am so excited I can hardly think straight. I ask Mark what we can do to get together with Kai.

Mark says he has a leave coming up. We will go to Georgia as soon as we have his exact location. We will all be a family at last. It has been so many years.

Kai may not want to see me! That thought strikes me as though a thunderbolt did. What if he won't see me? I deserted him and Tenika. *Oh, Kai and Tenika, can you find it in your heart to forgive me.*

Chapter 27

CUSTODY

Minton Hospital
Waiting for her mom to give birth
Susan

This woman came to me as I was sitting here in the hospital, waiting for my little brother or sister to be born. She told me that I would have to come with her. Mommy said I was never to go with strangers.

I said, "No, I won't." She took me by the hand, but I dragged my feet as she took me into a room.

"Be a big girl and listen to me," the woman says. "Your mother can no longer hear you crying. She is in heaven now."

I know about heaven. It is where dead people go if they are good. "Where is Mommy's baby, is he in heaven too?"

"No child, you have a little brother, and he is in the nursery."

"Can I see him?"

"You can in a little while. They have to clean him up, and the doctor has to check him first. Then, they will dress him and put him in an Isolette. You can see him through the window. I will take you there. I have some questions to ask you before we go there."

"Can I see my mommy? I want to see her. She told me to be good girl, and I have been a good girl, and I want to tell her that."

The woman is looking sad. I am sad too. I really do not understand, but I am trying to be good as Mommy said.

"Where is your dad?" the woman asks. "Do you know where he is?"

"I think he's in jail. Mommy said he was in jail, but I don't know where. Will he be coming to get me?"

"I don't think he can if he is in jail. Do you have a grandmother or grandfather or aunt or someone who can come get you?"

"I don't know. I have never seen anyone but Daddy and Mommy. My mommy said Kai was my baby brother's father."

"Who is Kai?"

"One of Mommy's boyfriends, I don't know his last name. He is not here anymore."

"Well," says the lady, "after we go see your baby brother, you will just have to come with me until will get this all figured out. I cannot just leave you here."

My baby brother is so little. I wish I could hold him. They tell me, no, he is too small, and children do not go into the nursery. Then they take me in a car to this woman's office.

Another woman comes along and tells me to come home with her. I will need to stay with her family until someone comes for me. I feel so lost and alone, and I want to be with my baby brother.

At the Prison
December 1
John

Calling Forsyth and telling them the situation, I have located Kai. A baby boy was born to Peggy. He is small and premature, but he is struggling to survive. Peggy was not so fortunate. She died of complications of eclampsia. They delivered the baby by C-section, and he is a few ounces less than five pounds. They found no other relative to take the baby. As soon as he is five and one-half pounds, they will release him from the hospital. Child Protective Services will take him until they find a home for him. Peggy has State Merit Insurance that is paying the hospital bill. Peggy told me Kai was the father. I do not know if he will admit to that. Lizzie and I went to see the baby, and he looks just like Kai. I have no doubt—it is his.

Peggy has a daughter, Susan. Peggy's ex-husband disappeared. I told them to check all the prisons. He seems to spend a good bit of his time in prison.

Defax (Division of Family and Children Services) took Susan, and she is in a foster home. Kai told me how much Elena hated being in foster homes.

I have Kai on the phone. "Kai, this is John, and I have some disturbing news. Peggy died in childbirth, and her baby boy is in the Minton Hospital. Peggy has always claimed that the baby is yours."

Stunned, Kai asks, "How is the baby? I did not think it was due yet. I am sorry about Peggy. I guess I should have kept in touch, but it has been a sticky situation with Elena and all."

"Lizzie and I went to see him. He is small but doing quite well. We think he looks just like you. How is Elena doing? Has she started to talk yet?"

"John, I am through here in two more days. When I get back to Elena, we will need to make a decision together. I am not leaving her out of the loop. My future is with Elena. I do not want the baby, *if it is mine*, in a foster home, but the decision is Elena's."

Atlanta
Two days later
Elena

Kai called and told Tanika that he will be home here Saturday. He asked to speak to me, but I want to wait and give him my letter myself and ask his forgiveness face-to-face. I would like to make this marriage work if he will have me. We have both been such fools. We belong together. I hope he will agree.

Tanika has been so good to me. I have been so fortunate to be able to take care of these babies for her. They are such beautiful boys. I wish they were mine. I long for a baby of my own. It has been ages since I have wanted anything else. Working in Atlanta is no longer my dream.

Saturday is here at last. Kai walks in the door, picks me up, and spins me around. He has tears in his eyes when he read my letter. I am crying too, as he holds me close and tells me he loves me.

I love you too, Kai, even if I have trouble saying the words. Someday, I will tell him, I promise myself. Someday, I will be able to say *all* the words.

Tanika has lunch ready, but neither Kai nor I eat much. Kai hugs his sister and tells her how much he has missed her. Kai says he has something important to discuss with us as a family. Tanika and I sit in the living room, each of us holding a twin.

Kai tells his story

"Elena and Tanika, I am not proud of what I have to tell you. Elena knew that Peggy was having a baby she claimed was mine. Well, the baby has been born. He is premature and in the Minton Hospital. Peggy, however, did not survive childbirth.

"I need to know what you think we should do. If that baby is mine, as Peggy said, I do not want him in a foster home, but it is up to Elena and you, Tanika, to give me advice. You two are my family. As a family, I would like us to make family decisions."

Elena takes a pencil and slowly writes what is in her mind. I wait expectantly as she painstakingly forms the words. "Kai, you know how I feel about foster homes. If that is your child, we should bring him home. That would be my decision." Elena looks at the baby in her arms and then at Tanika, who is sitting across from me, with a stern look on her face.

"Kai," Tanika scolds, "how could you do this to Elena? She has not told me a thing about your being unfaithful to her. I remember your wedding when you made all those promises. *Shame on you!*"

I am shaking now, upset by my sister's words. They are well deserved and I am ashamed.

"Tanika, Elena knows that I made a mistake, but she has forgiven me. I hope you will too. If Elena wants to go see that baby, could I borrow your car?"

"We will go together, Kai, Elena and I, to see this child. I will get the time off work, and we will go on Monday if that is all right with y'all. If this is a family problem, we will solve it as a family."

Elena Responding to the story

I remember that little red-haired girl I met in the doctor's office. "What about Peggy's little girl?" I write. "Where is she? Did her father pick her up?"

"She is in a foster home. They could not find her father."

Oh no, not that precious child! This has become too much for me, and I begin to cry. Kai comes to me and holds me in his arms as I continue to cry.

On the Road
Monday
Kai

Monday comes, and we all pile into Tanika's minivan. The twins are in their car seats in the middle with Tanika, and Elena and I are in the front. This will be quite a trip with the twins, but Tanika insists they need to go along. I do not argue. I am through arguing with anyone. All I want is to get this long journey over.

Finally, we are in Minton. We find a motel as the twins are tired from the long trip, and Tanika wants to rest with them. Elena and I go on to the hospital. They allow us to go to the maternity ward window to see the baby. As it is a small hospital, there are only two other babies in the nursery.

Elena picks out Peggy's child right away. He is red from crying. Elena knocks on the glass to get the nurse's attention. She motions she wants to see the baby, so they bring him up front right by the glass. Elena takes out her pen and notebook and writes furiously. "Kai, he looks just like you. That has to be your baby. How can we prove it?"

"That's a good question. We will need to find the social worker in charge to see what we can do. No one said this would be easy."

I talk with the hospital director who gives us the address of the Child Welfare Office. He tells us that the child will not be able to leave the hospital until he is over five pounds. That will probably take several more days. He seems to be a very helpful person. He probably would like to get this settled, so he can release the baby to someone.

Elena and I go back to the motel, and I talk to Tanika. The twins are sleeping peacefully now. They are all worn-out from their trip. I hope that Tanika can help us. She has worked for Defax in Atlanta for four years.

Tanika thinks she knows the answer. "First thing in the morning, we will go find the social worker in charge. Then we will need to get your blood test in order to establish paternity. It will not prove you are the father, but it will exclude you if you are not. We will need to find a judge that will award you temporary custody. That may take several days, but according to what you told me, we have a few days before the child is ready to go home. It will be much simpler if you can get the child released to you rather than from foster care."

"What about the little girl?" Elena is writing furiously. "What about Susan?"

"We don't have any claim on her," Tanika says. "It would be harder to get rights to her. Are you certain you want to, Elena?"

Elena is nodding her head and trying to talk. "Yes," she says. "Yes, yes, yes!"

Being it is a small town, the same caseworker has worked with both Susan, Peggy's daughter and Peggy's newborn son. She would like to see this case resolved, and she is very helpful, but doubtful that Susan can go with us. They have found Susan's father. He is in prison again at Odom, which is not that far away.

I take my blood test at the hospital. Then we call the prison in Odom and ask to have Susan's father call us. We will not be able to see a judge until the test comes back, so we go back to the motel and wait.

I am surprised when the phone rings, and the operator asks if I will accept a collect call from Odom. I answer, "Yes, ma'am. I will accept the charges."

Now that I have Ken on the phone, I have to make him listen to reason. Elena wants that child, and I will do my best to persuade him.

The inmate on the phone is sarcastic and asks, "What the hell do you want from me?"

"Well, sir, do you have a daughter, Susan?"

"What about it, I can't pay child support from in here."

"No, sir, we want to know if you will be claiming your daughter, she is in a foster home and needs our help."

"What's it to you? She ain't your kid."

I have to think fast. *What does this guy want?* "If we could adopt her, *you would not have to pay child support.*"

"I never wanted Susan. It was all Peggy's idea. How can I get out of supporting the brat? Where do I sign? She ain't nothing to me but a pain in the ass."

202

I am shocked at this, but I know Elena will be pleased. She wants both children. We seem to be making progress. Now, if we can get a judge to agree.

We have been here a week. The hearing will be on Tuesday. We have had an attorney make the petition for both children. We have gotten the signature from Susan's father, giving up all rights to Susan to Elena and me.

The caseworker has given her approval after a background check and the results of the blood test. Susan's foster parent brought her to the courthouse.

Susan is now seven years old, the same age as Elena was when she lost her parents. She takes Elena's hand and waits for the judge's decision. The judge gives temporary custody of both Peggy's baby and Susan to Elena and me. Elena is ecstatic. Tenika whispers, "It will take a while to make this permanent."

Susan seems to go along with the decision although she is very shy at first. She remembers Elena as that nice lady who has red hair just like she does. She recognizes me from the times I came to her house.

"Are you my baby brother's daddy?" she asks.

"I am going to be both your and your brother's dad if they will let me." I say, and Susan comes over and gives me a hug.

"I will like that," she says. "Will Elena be my new mommy?"

I let Elena answer that as Elena comes over and gives Susan a hug. I know Elena cannot say all the words. "Susan, Elena cannot talk right now, but I will say this for her, forever and ever, you will be our little girl and stay with your baby brother. We will all be one family. We will not leave you, I promise." Elena just beams at me as she holds Susan in her arms.

Susan smiles for the first time. In fact, everyone is smiling: the judge, the social worker, and the foster mom are all smiling and shaking our hands. It is the second best day of my life. Marrying Elena was the first. Now, if we can just get this family home. It will be a long trip with all these little people aboard. We still have to get my little son out of the hospital. I hope he is ready to meet his new mom and dad.

Chapter 28

THE LONG JOURNEY HOME

On the Road to Atlanta
December 14
Kai

The time has come to go back to Atlanta. We buy one more car seat for the baby. We pick up the baby from the hospital. Elena is excited and points to the blanket. It is the same yellow blanket that she knitted while she was waiting for our baby. He is dressed in part of the layette Elena sewed.

It is a bit crowded in the van. Our family now consists of the twins, the new baby, Susan, Tanika, Elena and me. Everyone is ready now as we start on the long journey home.

The babies are sleeping under the watchful eye of Susan, who reports excitedly of every move they make. We have to stop often, which makes the trip even longer, but no one is complaining.

Back in Marietta
The week before Christmas
Elena

Wow! Do I have a family! I knew I had to take both children. There was no way I could separate Susan from her little brother. Kai seems happy. Susan looks so much like me that I could be her real mother. I can hardly believe that little Michael Kai has the yellow blanket that I knitted. He has been a very good baby so far. This is my baby as much as if I had given birth to him. I was skeptical at first, but as he clings to me, I gaze on him with a mother's eyes. He looks so much like Kai.

Susan is thrilled to have a home. Traumatized by her experience in Minton when she thought she would not see her brother again, she clings to him possessively. She is a little shy with me and with Kai, but she loves all the babies, especially her baby brother she calls Mike.

I am going to work extra hard to try to talk. It will take awhile, but I need to communicate with these children. I can hug them and love them, but I need to be able to tell them how much.

Jerome has some news for us when we arrive home. He had a call from Tanika and Kai's mother, Mina. Mina has been searching for Kai for years and has finally found him.

Tanika was so excited that she called Mina and talked to her mother for hours. She found out that she has a brother, Flight, she did not know about, and a sister Regina. Mina, in turn, found out about Tanika's twins and of our journey to pick up these two little ones.

Kai hugs his sister and talks nonstop about his mother. He ignores all the rest of us, asking questions, and Tanika does her best to answer them. Tanika asks Kai to call his mother himself, but he says, "No. I will talk to her in person. I have many questions to ask her. I need to know why she left us and why she has not called us until now. I would like to meet my brother and sister and Mina's husband Mark.

It has been such a long time. I do not know my mother. Granny was always our mother. Mina was the one who left us. I will need to get some answers from Mina. I do not want to be hurt again. Growing up without her left a hurt that will be hard to get over, but if she can give me an explanation, I will be satisfied.

"Don't misunderstand me. I am as excited as everyone else is. I just need some answers."

Atlanta
December 19
Elena

Mina and her family are coming to Atlanta Christmas week. What a reunion that will be! I am so excited for Kai. I know he will be as happy to see Mina as the rest of us. She was lost to him, but now she has been found. I wish my mom and dad could see these lovely children. *Daddy and Mom, I love you. You have two beautiful grandchildren now. I hope we will have more in the years to come.*

Our season of discontent should be over now. All our prayers have been answered. Tanika has made us all very welcome here, but she knows we need our own home.

Kai and I have found a place three miles from Cartersville on Lake Aubrey in Bartow County. We will move our family there after Mina arrives. Susan will be in third grade. She is a very happy child now that we are all one family. Susan insists that Mike must sleep in her room. We let her have her way for now but tell her she must realize he will need his own room someday.

I know she misses her mommy, but she is adapting very well to our family. She has started to call Kai "Daddy." I hope she will one day call me "Mommy" as well. She is the little girl I have always dreamed of having.

Atlanta
Christmas, 1986
Kai

My mother is as beautiful as Granny had described her. She is tall and willowy. Her husband, Mark, is a likable person. I liked him from the first moment. He is shorter than Mina and quite a bit older. Flight and Regina are much lighter-skinned than Mina. They look more like their father than Mina. Both kids have golden brown hair. Regina's is short and curly. Flight has a crew cut like his dad.

Mina cried when she saw Tanika and me. Tanika cried when she met Flight and Regina. The twins, Jerry and Jerome, cried because they weren't the center of attention. Through all the tears, we are becoming acquainted.

I am so happy to see Mina that all my questions vanished. It does not really matter anyway. The past is the past. All of us have done things we regret, me most of all. We can only live life from this moment on. I hope to make the future the greatest!

Susan says, "My new granny," and sits on Mina's lap as though she belonged there. She has not left Mina's side since she came. Mina picks up baby Michael and holds him as though she is never going to let him go. While Mina is holding baby Michael, Susan keeps telling her, "That is *my* baby brother."

Jerry and Jerome are demanding attention. Tanika picks up Jerome, and Mina has Jerry. They are both sucking their thumbs and looking wide-eyed at Mina. "How do you tell them apart, they look so much alike?" Mina asks Tanika.

"Oh, they may look alike, but they both have different personalities. I may get confused when they are sleeping, but when they are awake I can tell. Jerry is the one you are holding. If he does not get his way, he screams. Jerome is a good boy and is easily satisficd. They both are hungry, most of the time. They seem to grow like weeds. Both of them were such long babies when they were born. I think they are going to be as tall as Kai."

While Mina admires all the babies, Mark is out in the yard playing with Flight and Regina. You can tell that they think the world revolves around their dad. It probably does. A dad was the one thing I missed most in life.

Time goes by so quickly. It seems they just got here and have to go again. We are sorry to see them pack up their children and get in the car to go back to North Carolina. Mark has to get back to base, but everyone agrees that this will just be the first of many visits.

Mina cries as she waves good-bye. Susan cries because Mina is leaving. The rest of us have tears in our eyes also. This has been a memorable visit. We all shed so many happy tears. So much hope is here for the future.

So long, Mina and Mark, we will miss you. It is time for us to get our things together to move to our new place in the country.

Lake Aubrey, Georgia
August 1987
Elena

Kai is working for the highway patrol, and he seem satisfied with the Cartersville assignment. He likes the post here and has made several friends already. This is an outstanding area to live in. Atlanta is within easy driving distance. We traded in the truck and bought a secondhand minivan like the one Tanika has. We need it now for our family.

I will never regret taking Peggy's children. They are my children now as though I had given birth to them. I will still remember my lost baby, but time is beginning to heal even that. It is my belief that my mom and daddy in heaven are raising that little soul. That thought comforts me.

When I think back on all that has happened to us, I am thrilled with what we have now accomplished.

I have regained most of my speaking ability. I have worked so hard to find all the words I need to express my feelings. Sometimes I have to speak slowly so that my mouth can catch up with my thoughts.

Simple pleasures have taken the place of childish dreams. Life at its worse is still worth the effort. Life at its best is the here and now.

We have the place Kai has always wanted: a place to live in the country but not too far from his sister Tanika.

I am happy to have a family. Atlanta is still there, but I am no longer enamored by the city. Being a mother makes me feel as important as I felt in Atlanta. The children need me, and I need them. Susan and Michael Kai are happy here. It is a place for them to grow.

I have another secret now. I am pregnant. I will tell Kai this evening. Then I will tell Susan and Michael. Susan loves babies, so she will be thrilled. Michael is still too young to understand that he will have a new playmate.

Life does not always give you a second chance. Kai and I now have that second chance. We are so lucky. In fairy tales, the prince and the princess live happily ever after. This is the happy ending Kai and I have always wanted.

Epilogue

Lake Aubrey, 2006

Hi, my name is Willow Mina Harjo. I was named after Kai, my father, and my grandmother Mina. What my mother, Elena, thought was a happy ending was just a happy beginning. Let me tell you the rest of the story.

I was born and raised in Bartow County near Cartersville, Georgia. My dad was in the highway patrol here until he retired a year ago. I have lived here all my life.

I have a sister, Susan Marie, whom Mom and Dad adopted when she was seven. She has been such a helpful sister not only to me but also to her baby brother, Mike. Mom named my brother Michael Kai Harjo after my grandfather Michael Kelley Mom's dad who died when mom was only seven.

Susan helped take care of us when we were little. She broke up the many disagreements that Mike and I had. As I got older, she became my best friend. We have always done everything together. We are so different. I have dusky skin just like my dad and long black hair. Susan has always braided it for me. She taught me how to dress and how to wear makeup when I got old enough.

Susan is a photographer's model. She has beautiful red hair and fair skin like my mother. When Susan smiles, it makes everyone smile, and she smiles almost constantly. Susan lives in Buckhead with her husband photographer Frank Penock and her daughter Penny. Penny is a mirror image of her mother. Susan has appeared in many magazines, sometimes with Penny. Everyone raves about both Penny and her mother. Both mother and daughter have that famous smile.

Mike is twenty. He is going to pre-med at Duke University in North Carolina. He is staying with Grandpa Mark and Grandma Mina, who are retired and living in Durham. They are very fond of Mike. He is an excellent student. Grandma Mina sometimes forgets and calls him "Kai."

Mike is so busy now with his studies, we rarely see him except at Christmas when the entire clan gets together.

I am two years younger than Mike. Both Mike and I look like our father Kai. Mike is not as tall as Kai, but I have grown tall and slim like the willow tree. I am not as beautiful as my sister Susan is, but I am not ugly either.

Our farm, surrounded by a stand of southern loblolly pines that stretch their dark green branches skyward almost one hundred feet, is in Bartow County bordering Lake Aubrey. These giant trees whisper in the wind as though gossips with a secret. The deer they shelter come up right into our yard. Red fox, squirrels, and possum run through our woods. Lake Aubrey is full of fish. As children, we fished with cane poles and worms, impatiently waiting for a fish to bite on our hooks, pushing and shoving, and making enough noise to scare away any fish in the vicinity. We skipped rocks across the water, and waded in the shallows.

We played hide-and-seek among the willows. Mike was the rowdy one, always climbing up the pine trees and swinging like Tarzan on ropes he had attached to the branches. As he grew older, he built a tree house that he and the neighbor boy Robby used as a clubhouse. *Girls not allowed* according to Mike, but we sometimes climbed up there when the boys were not looking. Mike, encouraged by our father, considers himself a true Native American. Kai and Mike made bows from willow branches and shot arrows at whatever poor squirrel might wander in their path.

Now that Dad has retired, Dad and I spend most of our time raising many varieties of trees. All the trees grow well around the lake where we live. Willows love water. Our soil seems to be just right for them. We played under the willows as children. The wind blowing in the willows makes such a rustling sound that they seem to be singing. At night, they sing a lullaby to help us fall asleep.

My grandmother, Mina, told me the story of Grandpa Willow Tree. We still live in His shadow. When Grandma Mina visited in Cartersville, she gave Mom cuttings from the original willow. A willow grew for each child, both Susan and Mike. I came along later, so Mom just broke off a branch of Susan's willow and planted it for me. That is what is so neat about willow trees. They grow easily and quickly.

We sell some willows that began with Grandpa Willow Tree although we grow all types of trees and shrubs and ship them all over the South.

My favorite tree is, of course, the willow of which we grow several varieties that are perfect for our growing zone, which is seven. Prairie willows grow this far south, as well as black willows (my favorite), and weeping willows.

Some of my other favorite trees are purple ash, horse chestnut, flowering pear, autumn blooming cherry, black walnut, and Chickasaw plum. We have magnolias and many flowering shrubs. Our clay soil is perfect for all these and makes root balls easily for transplanting.

My dad says I have a green thumb when it comes to growing things. I think he is right. Maybe it is just because I talk to all the trees and plants.

They seem to grow better when I talk to them. Dad says I am just like my great-grandmother Niabi Harjo. After hearing the tale of this generous Native American woman, I know that this is Dad's highest compliment.

We have several quarter horses on our small farm. We all know how to ride. Mom takes care of the barn while Dad and I spend more time in the tree orchard.

When Susan was home, she rode in some of the local barrel races. Her quarter horse was a mare she named Feathers after mom told her the story about how she called the mane on her mare "feathers." Feathers is a strong horse, fast and dependable. She responds well to the reins and makes a perfect barrel racer. When Susan was little, she was upset when Mom told her she could not sleep in the barn with her horse.

Feathers is getting very old now and not as agile as she used to be. We still ride her some, but her barrel racing days are over. She has given us several foals. Some of which we have kept, but most of them we sold. Mom hated to see any of them go. They are all beautiful quarter horses.

My favorite horse is a spirited two-year-old colt named Chili Pepper. Mom and I can ride Chili Pepper, but he does not like Dad. He lays back his ears, snorts and pitches a fit if Dad tries to get on. I laugh but Dad does not see the humor in it. Chili Pepper really lives up to his name.

My aunt Tanika and Jerome still live in Atlanta. Their twin sons, Jerome and Jerry, played basketball in high school. Both boys are almost seven feet tall. They are both attending law school at Emory University in Atlanta. Mom thinks they will be good lawyers. She says it is because they cried so much as babies. They have always been smart, always asking questions no one could answer. In addition, Mom said that everyone would have to look up to them as tall as they are.

My uncle Flight, Mark and Mina's younger son and Kai and Tanika's little brother, is in the air force. He is a pilot who has flown many missions in Iraq. He is currently based overseas at Ramstein Air Base in Germany.

Mina hopes he will be able to come home soon. Mark is convinced that his son is a hero and needs to serve his country wherever they send him.

Flight's sister Regina Fawn is married to an MD who teaches at Duke University Medical School where Mike is attending. Regina is the only tiny one in the family. I tower over her when we get together. Regina has brown trusting eyes like a doe. Her skin is the color of buckskin and her hair is a golden brown. I must admit I envy her coloring. Both Flight and Regina Fawn are unique in their ability to charm the rest of us. The entire family cannot wait to be in their presence.

Dad and I have different ideas about the best ways to do things, but when we do argue, it is with mutual respect for each other's opinions.

One of our arguments is about the way we keep bees. Dad thinks he knows more about how to care for the bees than I do. I have been studying all the material on the Internet to find the very best ways to nurture our bees. He believes that some of the older ways are best.

Either way our beehives are some of the finest in the state. The bees help pollinate our flowering shrubs and furnish us with honey that we sell. Raising bees is frustrating, especially now as it is sometimes difficult to keep the hives healthy and well. The frustration is worth it, I think. I take my honey to the state fair every year. I have won several blue ribbons.

My hobby is poetry. I write a poem every day. Some of them are better than others are. It depends upon my mood. I have written poems ever since I was a little girl. If I keep writing enough, Mom says, my style will improve. I wrote this one for Mom and Dad after they told me the story of their difficult times. Every marriage has problems sometimes. My point is that love will endure if it is strong enough.

Mom wants me to go to college and pursue a career, but I feel more at home, here with my trees and my parents Kai and Elena.

Mom told me she was a word processor. I think of myself as a word gatherer here on my computer. We are miles apart now in technology from where Mom started. In just a few short years, the Internet has become a tool. I cannot imagine a world without it.

I do not want to leave this place. When I am ready, I will marry and raise a family here where I spent my happy childhood. We will raise our bees, flowers and trees together as a family. When Kai and Elena grow old, we will care for them in the shadow of the willows. This is my destiny, I think, here among the other willows.

LOVE IS

Love is a whisper
softly in your ear
your heart like a pom-pom
just bursting with cheer.

Love is a smile
you can never erase
permanently glued
all over your face.

Love is a gesture
that took lots of thought
it's about what is given
not what you got.

Love is a memory
etched deep in you brain
when the fighting is over
it will always remain

Love is like sunshine
helping your heart grow
it weathers the storm
wherever you go.

Love is like a flower
with a bee's tender care
unfolding all that it touches
and lingering there.

Love is so wonderful
when it starts anew
and lasts through the years
it reminds me of you.

Love, willow

TIME LINE

1838   Trail of Tears

1865   Civil War

1880   Flight Harjo is born.

1893   Granny is born.

1942   Mina is born.

1956   Flight Harjo dies in North Carolina at age seventy-six.

1957   Mina is fifteen and pregnant.

1958   Mina gives birth to Tanika.

1959   Mina at eighteen gives birth to Kai and runs off.

1960   Elena is born.

1967   Elena is seven and orphaned.

1969   Mina, twenty-seven, joins the air force.

1972   Mina, thirty-two, and Mark are married.

1972   Kai's father dies, and Kai moves to Missouri.

1977   Kai joins the marines.

1979   Mina, thirty-seven, is discharged from the air force.

1981   An assassin shot the Polish pope four times.

1981   Attempt to assassinate President Reagan.

1981   Tanika and Jerome get married.

1981   Flight is three.

1981   Granny dies in Missouri at eighty-eight.

1981   Elena starts working for Irv.

1982   The Falkland Island is invaded by Argentina.

1983   June, Kai is discharged from the marines.

1983   Sally Ride became the first American woman in space.

1983   October, Flight is five, Mina and Mark are in North Carolina Mina is pregnant with Regina Fawn.

1984   Kai, twenty-three, and Elena, twenty-four, get married. Kai and Elena living on state reservation

1985   Elena is hurt and loses baby.

1985   Kai goes to Forsyth for highway patrol training.

1986   Peggy dies, leaving Susan and baby orphaned. Susan and baby Michael Kai Harjo are adopted.

1986   USSR launches the famous Mir Space Station.

1986   Mina and Mark and Flight and Regina Fawn, Tanika and Jerome and twins, Elena and Kai and Susan and Michael Kai find each other.

1988   Willow Mina is born to Elena and Kai.

2006   Willow finishes the story.

Read on for an excerpt of *Willow Mina* coming soon from the author of *The Willow Tree*.

WILLOW MINA

SUMMER REDFERN

Note from the Author

Willow Mina is the second in a series about the Harjo family.

This is a preview of a novel continuing the saga of Willow Mina daughter of Kai Harjo and Elena. It should be ready to publish sometime in 2009.

To the Mound Builders

In cadence with ancient drums, I walk
along this foot-worn path
in reverence listening
as winds rustling through the forest, talk.

Here upon this hallowed ground
Etowahan feet once trod
a vanished nation gone save only this mysterious mound.

Spirits hover in this sacred plane
faint echoes still resound
from dust again to dust
only relics by the creek remain.

What eternal purpose shall *we take*,
leaving our mortal sphere,
as dust again to dust
what difference will *our journey make*?

Love, Willow

Prologue

The wind in the willows is singing our song. The ancient chants of my ancestors resound through the forest as clearly now as they did before I was born. I hear the drum beat, in sync with my heart. Voices hushed by the silence of time whisper my name, "Willow Mina Harjo, beloved daughter of the forest, come dance." It is here that I belong, beneath the other willows.

My name is Willow and this is my story. The story I finished for my parents, Kai and Elena Harjo, was the beginning of mine.

I rise early each morning and come silently on moccasin-clad feet to watch the glorious sunrise along the border of our lake. The gentle lapping of the water over the moss-covered-granite rocks give a cadence to the song created by the breeze that sings through the loblolly pines that reach skyward into the heavens. Their dark shapes seem darker still against the pale crimson dawn. As I sway with the wind, I feel the morning mist softly caressing my face, and dripping noiselessly from the leaves as I stand here with the rest of my kin. I hold out my arms in supplication to the rising sun, whose beams glisten in the mist on every leaf, as it slowly rises to awake the creatures of this forest that are sleeping under its sheltering boughs.

As the day begins, the rustling of the leaves whisper of a former time when the mound builders of the Etowah stood here on this hallowed ground, around this lake and in this forest, murmuring in their native tongue. I feel their spirits in the stillness of this place. They are all around me, their ghostly presence awakening in me a reverence for my native land.

I know this Earth does not belong to me, that I belong to it. The Great Spirit loaned it to me as I shall loan it to my children and they to theirs. I shall return to the dust, as did my ancestors before me. This thought comforts me as I return to my home beside this lake to begin my daily chores.

CHAPTER 1

BESIDE THE LAKE

April 25, 2006

"Willow, is that you?" Kai's sharp eyes discern a slight movement through the trees as he rocks impatiently back and forth on the swing hanging on the porch.

Retirement from the Highway Patrol has left him restless. Kai rises early, unable to stay in bed with the sleeping Elena, who neither is an early riser now that the children are grown, nor is she as agile as her husband is.

"Willow" Kai calls again.

"Hi, Dad, ready for our run?"

An answer to that is not necessary, as both my father and I follow the same routine each morning. Our long legs reach a comfortable stride as we round the corner of the Cabin to follow the foot-worn path over the purple-tinged mountain barely visible through the mist that surrounds it.

I am still in my reverie with my ancestors and wonder how many of them passed this way. I glance at my dad and marvels at his stamina as he runs as effortlessly as a panther while I, winded, am slowing slightly while stubbornly trying to match his pace. (Dad is forty-seven and six feet, seven inches tall. I am eighteen and six feet, two inches tall).

As I look up a large bird falls from the sky. I listen carefully but hear no gun report. *I wonder what happened to it*, I ponder. *This seems significant.* I close my eyes and reach deep into my mind but am not able to see the event this forebodes. Lately I have been either having visions of events that have happened or are about to occur. I wonder if these are merely coincidental or if I have some special sense.

A fawn runs across our path as we return to the lake. *Was that Niabi my great-grandmother? (Niabi is Osage for fawn.)* I have seen that fawn before and had a vision of my great-grandmother then. I feel the spirit of Niabi again but I do not know how to communicate with it. Maybe my grandmother Mina will know. I will send her an e-mail, I muse.

Breakfast is ready as we return to the cabin. Eggs, buttermilk biscuits with sawmill gravy, and the every present grits complete the feast that my mother Elena has prepared.

Conspicuously absent from this fare is the country ham or bacon usually served by southern cooks, but omitted by Elena. She has not eaten nor served meat since she worked in the dairy in south Georgia some twenty years ago after learning how cruelly they butcher the animals. Even the sawmill gravy has been modified from the usual ham drippings. Our family although on a modified vegetarian diet has thrived. Kai, prefers a meat-filled diet, but only eats meat when Elena is not present. He has learned not to cross his determined wife.

Elena seems astonished at the appetite of both dad and me. We both eat ravenously and still stay miraculously trim, while she must constantly watch her weigh.

I used to be so thin, almost too thin when I was in south Georgia, she thinks. I have always had a thin image of myself.

Missing from the table is my brother Mike who is working in Durham, North Carolina and is living with Mina our grandmother while he attends medical school.

The phone is ringing as Mom and I are clearing the table. Kai jumps up to answer it, listens to the voice on the other end and almost drops the phone. "Elena there has been an accident!"

"Did you say accident, who?" is Elena's query, afraid to ask as she envisions one of her children.

"It must be Flight!" I worry. "My uncle Flight has flown several missions to Iraq, but he is stationed in Germany, I thought he was safe there."

I am deeply saddened, as Flight is a favorite of mine. I have sent him e-mails at least three times a week, and he has always responded to me his favorite niece.

"I have not heard from him since last week, but I just thought he was busy or something."

"It *is* my brother Flight!" Kai questions, "Willow how did *you* know?"

"I had a vision, Dad," I reply, "When I saw that bird fall from the sky I knew it represented something although at the time I could not determine what it was. Then that fawn was there so I felt it must concern our family."

"I don't see what that fawn had to do with it. I saw it too, but it was just a fawn."

"No, dad, don't you see that was Niabi. I could feel her presence."

Mina, Kai and Flight's mother, is on the phone, but she does not have any details yet, only that he is in a hospital in Germany.

I run to my computer, always a source of my knowledge, to see what I can discover.

"A plane crashed yesterday in Afghanistan" I announce, "It was carrying a crew of four and some U.S. narcotics agents. Maybe he was piloting that one. It says the U.S. leased it and had a military crew out of Ramstein airbase. That is where Flight is. Two of the crew died in the crash, and two crewmembers survived. All of the twelve narcotics agents survived although there were some injuries. That is all I can find out here."

I quickly check my e-mail, but find nothing from Flight or Mike this morning. Closing my eyes, I envision my injured uncle. *He is lying so still.*

"I think he is unconscious!" I exclaim.